ECHO

BY

RON ROHRBAUGH, JR.

Author's Note:

This book is a work of fiction that is inspired by actual history, people, and places. For example, Chief Woapalanne (Bald Eagle) was a Lenape tribal leader who lived near Milesburg, PA and is believed to have killed James Brady, the brother of famous frontiersman Sam Brady. Renovo and Young Woman's Creek are real places in Clinton County, PA, and elk still roam the Pennsylvania Wilds. While many Native Americans were pushed from their homeland, the story itself, including the existence of the Elk Eater Band, is a product of my imagination.

In the telling of this story, I tried my best to use the proper names of plants and animals, and to describe wilderness survival techniques in accurate detail. This work is fiction, but it could have happened, just as I describe it. Natural history and outdoor pursuits are magical and I hope this book inspires you to get outside and learn more.

My intent is to be respectful of ALL people and cultures. This can be difficult, given that some names and terms are inaccurate or have taken on negative connotations. There is no perfect solution. In this book, I have chosen to use "Native American" and "Indian" interchangeably when referring to the people who inhabited this continent when Europeans first arrived. The term "Indian" is used universally in the historical record and continues to be accepted by many contemporary native peoples.

In Chapter 14, the Native American sayings related to weather were adapted from The Frontiersmen by Allan W. Eckert (1967).

For more information, please contact me at:
916 E. Mountain Rd, Port Matilda, PA 16870

RonRohrbaugh@gmail.com

ISBN: 9798521355563

Dedication:

To Rex and Leela, our adventures and your overflowing joy fill my heart and inspire my creativity. Thank you! With great love and admiration, Dad.

Acknowledgement:

Writing a book while the rest of your busy life spins around you is one of the more difficult intellectual challenges one can face. I am deeply grateful for my wife, Debbie, who always makes "space" for my creative yearnings and provides insightful, unvarnished feedback to keep me on the right path.

THE
PENNSYLVANIA WILDS

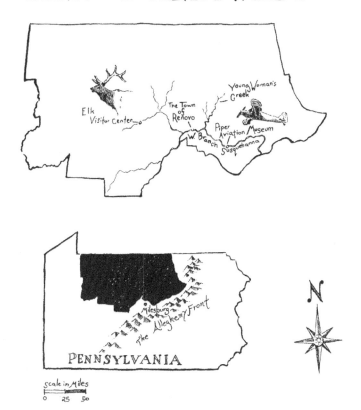

Elk Visitor Center

The Town of Renovo

Young Woman's Creek

Piper Aviation Museum

W. Branch Susquehanna

Milesburg

The Allegheny Front

PENNSYLVANIA

N

scale in Miles

0   25   50

1

ALONE

Thursday, October 14th

9:37 a.m.

Echo forced his eyes open. It took effort, something like arching his eyebrows, just to get his eyelids to follow along. He knew something, maybe everything, was wrong. He sensed that he was on his back, looking up, but could see only straight up. Nothing to the sides, just straight up, like he was looking through two empty toilet paper rolls. Above him were intertwined shapes against a dingy gray background. The indistinct shapes looked like loose spaghetti or maybe one of those Rorschach tests he just learned about in his sixth-grade science class.

Then, BAM! His vision cleared all at once and a thousand senses bombarded his brain: The earthy smell of decomposition. The sound of distant migrating geese arguing about the lead flock position. A nearby Yellow-bellied Sapsucker tapping out its distinctive Morse code on some dead branch. His mouth was gummy and tasted like the time he'd face-planted from the monkey bars while showing off on the school playground. The spaghetti, or Rorschach blotches, or whatever they were came into focus as tree branches outlined against a gray sky that would soon spit rain or maybe snow. Yes, that confirmed it; he was on his back in the forest.

He twisted his head, hearing the leaves crunch under his skull as they slid through his blonde hair. There, ten feet away and leaning against the big white pine, was his hickory longbow, just where he'd left it before deciding to climb up. And closer, not far from his hip . . . what was that black fragment on the ground? He pinched his eyes shut and reopened them, glad he could now see, but frightened by the sight. The fragment was a piece of his lifeline, or what used to be his lifeline. The black housing of the two-way radio his parents insisted he bring lay shattered, its electronic guts spread out a few inches away.

Next to take hold were his nerve endings. His right ankle throbbed with a dull ache, and even without touching it, he could feel that it was swollen with the blood of broken vessels. His neck and face were not right either. They stung like a thousand yellow jackets had been at him. *What in the world had happened?* he wondered.

The distinct memories would come later, but for the moment, he knew this was bad. Very bad. It was just a little after eight o'clock in the morning. He had already made his daily call home, so no one would be worried for at least twenty-four hours. He needed water, food, and probably medical attention. The water was in his backpack, but the fifteen feet between him and the pack seemed like a mile. *Just one thing at a time*, he thought, but then panic started to come.

He breathed hard, short breaths and clammy sweat beaded against the skin of his neck. "Get ahold of yourself," he said aloud. "You're an Orion and you're going to be a Sure Enough Mountain Man." *What to do? What to do?* he thought. Assess the situation. That's what his dad and Uncle Leo would say. There's opportunity in every situation, you just have to find it. *The bow*, he thought. *At least I have the bow.* The sight of it, the knowledge of what he could do with it and what he'd learned by making it brought him some calm, but it didn't last. "Why wasn't I more careful?" he admonished.

It was the hunger. The gnawing hunger. Food, he knew, drove the natural world like nothing else. Energy from the sun supported plants that were eaten by herbivores like cotton-tailed rabbits, which eventually became the poop of carnivores like red foxes. He knew all of this and more from the books in his own natural history library and the documentaries he'd seen. Like the one about life on the African plains, where baby zebras got snapped up like oyster crackers during river crossings by hungry crocodiles. It had taken a few days, but he was now part of that natural world, part of a system driven by constant hunger, and he had taken a foolish risk for food.

A thought of home, his mom, and the smell of taco Tuesday flashed in his mind. The shattered two-way radio stared back at him as if mocking him, like a single square tooth from a rotten jack-o-lantern.

I'm alone, he thought. Utterly alone! A lump burst into his throat and before he could swallow it, hot tears boiled in his eyes and rolled down his cheeks. He screamed, "HELP! Dad, get me the heck out of here!" The screams might as well have been whispers. There was no one to hear him amid the deep forest and gurgling sounds of Young Woman's Creek, miles from the nearest road or house.

2

Z-BUCK

Friday, January 15th

3:30 p.m.

Echo darted from the school bus as he yelled, "See you Monday," to his friend and sometimes enemy Buster Brasher. Like the Orions, Buster's family loved the outdoors, and they spent a lot of time camping, hunting, and fishing. But Echo didn't always agree with the way they did things. Echo's family had a deep respect for nature that Buster's family didn't seem to care much about. This rubbed Echo the wrong way and sometimes led to scuffles between the two boys.

Echo jumped from the bus's bottom step and immediately fell hard on his butt as his feet lost traction on the icy driveway. He could hear Buster roaring with laughter and yelling from inside the school bus. "Smooth move, Mr. Graceful. Don't try out for the gymnastics team!" hollered Buster. Echo shook himself off, threw a look at the departing bus, and started trudging up the long, wooded driveway to his family's log cabin. The closer he got, the faster he walked.

He burst through the back door, encountering his mom, Olivia Orion, who gave him a puzzled look. "What's the hurry, Echo?" she asked.

"Mom, I've got two hours before dark, and I think I've figured out where Z-Buck has been bedding. I want to search for his shed antlers before squirrels chew them up. I really want them for my natural history collection."

It was early January, and white-tailed deer bucks were dropping their antlers for the season. In a remarkable biological feat, all members of the deer family, even moose with antlers weighing up to seventy-five pounds, have evolved to lose their old antlers and regrow new ones every year. The cost of carrying heavy antlers through the difficult winter is greater than the energy needed to regrow new ones each spring. Finding a shed antler was like finding a little piece of the deer's energy, and Echo loved to search for them.

"And where is it you think old Z-Buck is sleeping?" asked Echo's mom.

"Up on Chestnut Flats," mumbled Echo.

"Where?" she asked sternly.

"Chestnut Flats," Echo said more clearly.

"Echo, that's a thirty-minute hike, and you know how easy it is to get lost up there."

"I know, Mom, but it's supposed to snow tomorrow, and I can't find shed antlers under the snow. Please, may I go?"

The left side of Olivia Orion's face started to curl up, and instantly Echo began a victory dance, with his hands waving high above his head. In his eleven years on Earth, he had figured out ways to predict his parents. When she was about to say yes, his mom's left cheek did a little upward twitch, and Echo knew he was in! Echo gave her a quick hug, changed into warm clothes, and tossed some water and an apple in his school pack. He paused before going through the back door and said, "See you at dark, Mom.

The Orions lived in Pennsylvania at the base of Moshannon Mountain on the Allegheny Front. Their cabin sat in the woods on the edge of a vast wilderness called the Pennsylvania Wilds, where elk, bear, and some said even mountain lions still roamed. All of this was Echo's backyard. Chestnut Flats lay at the top of the ridge behind his house.

Echo was following a faint deer trail up the steep ridge and stopped for a break as the trail leveled out on Chestnut Flats. He pulled the apple from his pack and leaned back on a big chestnut oak tree that had deeply furrowed bark like an alligator's hide. While he ate, Echo glanced around for landmarks that could guide him back to this spot on his way home. He knew how tricky it could be hiking on flat ground in the forest. On a ridge, you could keep your sense of direction by simply going up or down. It was kind of like going upstream or downstream on a river.

A "flat" didn't work that way. If you lost your sense of direction in flat forest, you could wander in circles for days without some sort of landmark, like a distant mountain or the position of the sun to guide you. On this gray day, Echo would have no sun to determine which way was north, or any other direction for that matter. *I have to pay attention to my surroundings*, Echo thought to himself.

Echo took the last bite of apple and began sneaking toward what he knew to be the thickest part of Chestnut Flats. His eyes scanned the forest floor for the white-brown color and tapered shape of a deer's shed antler. "Sheds," as collectors called them, were difficult to see, and it took practice to get good at finding them.

Echo knew that having a mental search image was everything when trying to identify something in nature. The Germans called it *gestalt*, or something like that. It was the idea that you could see just a tiny part of something, like the feather of a bird or the scale of a fish, yet know exactly what the whole thing was. If he was going to find one of Z-Buck's shed antlers, he had to imprint the look of that antler in his mind's eye. *A piece of cake*, he told himself. Echo had first seen Z-Buck on an October morning when "Z" was just two years old, and Echo himself only nine.

He was waiting for the school bus when a buck burst from the woods across the road and screeched to a halt mere feet from Echo. Its medium-sized, eight-point rack was nothing special, except for one defining feature—the longest tine on the left antler was shaped like a perfect letter *Z*. That February, Echo found Z's left antler, which was now a treasured specimen in his natural history collection. Though Echo saw Z in their woods several times over the years, he could not find another of his sheds. Perhaps this year would be different.

Suddenly, a streak of white and brown flashed on the trail straight ahead. The deer crashed through the brush, running deeper into Chestnut Flats. *Gotcha!* Echo said to himself. He knew it must be a buck, maybe even Z. Echo had an intense curiosity about animals and wondered where the deer would go. *I have to track it*, he thought. With his head down, focusing on the deer's tracks, Echo was paying too little attention to his surroundings. Before long, towering rhododendron shrubs with branches resembling twisted arms swallowed him like a crowd at the state fair.

Back at home, Echo's mom was staring out of the kitchen window into the darkening woods. She was worried. Echo should have been back by now. Everyone knew Olivia Orion judged darkness—and the need to have your butt home—not by the clock, but by how well she could see the granddaddy white oak that grew at the edge of the clearing. She hadn't been able to see the oak for fifteen minutes and was becoming more anxious by the second. Echo was very capable for eleven, but he sometimes lacked the good sense that experience provides. She turned off the kitchen light, hoping to see Echo's flashlight on the trail leading down from the mountain, but there was only blackness.

She snapped the light back on and was just turning her attention back to the fish frying on the stove when Rachel, Echo's older sister, came marching down the hall. "Mom! What stinks? Are you burning something?" Rachel asked. "You know all the cooking smells drift into my room, and I'm trying to read a new book on climate change for school."

"Sorry, dear," said Olivia. "It's just that Echo's not back yet."

"Oh, don't worry," blurted Rachel. "You know Echo. He's probably out looking for sign of that mysterious buck of his again."

Just then, the back door popped open and Olivia's heart jumped as she wheeled around, expecting to see Echo. Her face dropped when she saw her husband, Ted, stride through the door. "Ted, thank goodness you're home. Echo went up on the mountain to look for Y-Buck's shed antlers and he's not back yet."

Ted grinned a little and said, "It's Z-Buck not Y-Buck."

"Whatever!" Olivia said. "The point is, Echo is out in the dark with a storm coming."

Ted reassured Olivia and Rachel that Echo would be fine, saying, "Echo knows those woods as well as I do. He knows what to do." Olivia wasn't convinced and let out a worried sigh. Promising his wife he'd go look for Echo, Ted hopped in his truck with a quick goodbye and drove the dirt roads over the mountain to reach Chestnut Flats as quickly as possible.

Soon, big, wet snowflakes began falling like slush balls onto the Orions' back porch. For nearly two hours, Olivia paced the floor and Rachel pretended to read her climate change book. Then, a flash of headlights, moving painfully slow, began creeping up the driveway.

"Mom, that's not Dad's truck," yelled Rachel.

Olivia had time to pull on her coat and walk to the driveway before the truck reached the house. The truck was big and old, with rust all over the green paint and a blue fiberglass cap that didn't match the rest of the vehicle.

When the driver's door opened, out popped old Luna Woapalanne—tall and angular, with long salt-and-pepper hair to her shoulders, dressed in dirty men's overalls. Luna was all business. The interior light revealed a sheepish Echo sitting awkwardly in the passenger's seat. "Found this here 'un huddled around a fire, burning his homework up on Chestnut Flats. Says he lives here." She continued without a break, "Right smart kid to strike a warming fire with paper, but that ain't no natural smell. Stench of it led me right to him. Don't have time for small talk; my boys caught a whiff of coon on the flats and we need to get back." Olivia could hear coon dogs barking feverishly from beneath the truck's blue cap. Echo jumped down from the truck and moped to his mom's side. Luna closed the ancient truck's door with a bang and bounced down the driveway as Olivia yelled "Thank you" into the wind.

The bark of coon dogs had no more than disappeared when Echo's dad pulled up the driveway. He got out, hugged Echo tight, and then held him by the shoulders. Ted looked into Echo's eyes and gently said, "Where were you, son? What were you thinking?"

"He's freezing, Ted. We can talk about this later. Let's get him in the house," said Echo's mom.

Echo went straight to his room for dry clothes while his parents discussed the situation. After fifteen minutes, Echo still had not returned. Ted walked down the hall to Echo's room, expecting to find him going over his natural history collection, but instead he discovered an exhausted Echo facedown and sound asleep under a mountain of blankets.

When Ted returned to the living room, Rachel said, "Dad, what do you make of that crazy Luna Woapalanne? The kids at school call her Looney Luna!"

Ted thought of saying what he really thought, but instead, he simply said, "There's more to her than meets the eye, but let's leave it until morning. Echo needs to hear it too."

3

NEEDLE IN A HAYSTACK

Thursday, October 14th

9:56 a.m.

When nothing but the wind replied to his desperate calls for help, Echo crawled first to his hands and knees and then attempted to stand. "No can do," screamed his right ankle, as even the slightest weight on the joint sent shock waves of pain up his leg. He now sat with his left leg in a half "criss-cross applesauce" position and his right leg extended straight in front of him. With each jolt of pain, his stomach flipped like a thousand roller-coaster rides. He felt himself go cold and threw up what little his stomach held onto the oak and maple leaves between his legs. Wiping his mouth with the sleeve of his coat, he bent forward to look at his foot. It was swelling before his eyes, and he felt his boot laces cutting into his skin. He reached for the belt knife on his left hip, but there was nothing there but an empty sheath. The knife must have been torn out during the fall. Then he remembered the chert neck knife that he was told to always wear as a symbol of strength, a way to remind himself that he could do anything. The stone knife was small, but its serrated edge was sharp enough to skin a bear.

Echo reached between his many layers of clothing and pulled the knife up through the neck of his shirt and over his head. The rawhide lace and small sheath of soft deerskin were warm from his body and held the fragrance of animal hide. Gripping the knife's wood handle, he nicked the lace near its knot, and his boot flung open from the pressure of his swelling foot. The new blood rushing to his foot brought excruciating pain, and he wanted to saw the whole dang boot off rather than tug to remove it. Instead, he sat a moment with the pain, letting big tears silently roll down his cheeks. He needed to save the boot and its lace as they were imperative to his survival. Tug! Stifled scream! Tug! Stifled scream! Tug! Stifled scream!

The boot fell free. He peeled the wool sock from his foot and breathed a short sigh.

The sight of his bloated, purple foot reminded him of the blowfish he had caught while fishing in the ocean with his Uncle Leo. When in danger, blowfish puff themselves to triple their size to ward off predators. Leo had told Echo to stay clear of the fish's mouth, but Echo ignored his uncle and decided to just tickle the fish's rigid lips with his index finger. In an instant, the sandpapery mouth slammed shut on little Echo's finger like a set of vice-grip pliers. Blood spurted from the finger and then trickled down Echo's wrist. Leo chuckled, and at the time, it made Echo mad and embarrassed, but now he smiled at the memory and wished Leo was with him now. Uncle Leo was an expert woodsman and as close to a modern mountain man as you could get.

The cold, damp earth felt good on Echo's foot, and he piled wet leaves from the forest floor on top of it. Soon he felt better, and skootching backward on his butt and hands, he made his way to the big white pine where his hickory bow leaned. On the way, he grabbed his backpack, dragging it behind him. Resting against the giant tree's trunk, Echo took a long drink from his water bottle. Cool water never tasted so good, and his brain began to clear from what must have been a mild concussion.

Lashed to the outside of his pack was a smooth, gray American beech stick with five grooves carved around it like rings. Five. That was the number of mornings he had woken up in the woods. The plan for this "Sure Enough Mountain Man" trip had been simple. It was a six-day hike through the Pennsylvania Wilds. Yes, he would be alone, but as long as he stuck to the plan, he would be alright.

His mom and dad had dropped him off at the Elk Rock trailhead on Saturday morning, with a plan to pick him up the following Friday at one of their favorite spots near a big swamp. He would sleep under the stars for six nights and cover fourteen miles across numerous ridges and creek drainages. It would be like nothing Echo had ever done—a way to prove himself as a true mountain man.

As he left the parking area and trekked into the woods alone, inside he felt like Jell-O, but outwardly he kept a steely composure, telling his mom and dad "not to worry."

His mom yelled to him, "Echo, I love you. Use your head, and call me every morning on the two-way radio like we planned."

If Echo heard her voice crack, he didn't acknowledge it. He just thrust his right hand into the air as if to say, "Got it, Mom; I know the plan," and kept walking until he was out of sight. Just a kid hiking toward manhood.

That was the plan. The plan. The plan. The plan. "Stick to the plan," his dad preached. "Stick to the plan, and if anything goes wrong, we'll be able to find you. If you don't stay near the trail, it'll be like finding a needle in a haystack." Echo couldn't believe how stupid he was. He hadn't stuck to the plan . . . .. in fact not even close. He was miles off the trail with a broken radio and a badly injured leg. He was a tiny needle in a giant wilderness haystack!

4

THE CONVERSATION

Saturday, January 16th

8:11 a.m.

Echo awoke to breakfast dishes clanking in the kitchen. He lay in his bed, fingers laced behind his head. There was another sound too—a more rhythmic one. It was a whispered disagreement between his parents. He only caught snatches of words. He heard his mom say, "Yes, but that's the point. He's not a Mountain Man. He's an eleven-year-old boy."

"He'll be almost twelve by the time of our trip," replied Echo's dad.

"What's the difference? He's still a kid," insisted Oliva.

Ted spoke louder now. "Every Orion since my great grandfather's time has proven himself on a wilderness trip before his first hunting season."

"Don't you mean every *boy*," replied a stern Olivia. "Rachel hunts, and she never became a Sure Enough Mountain Man, as you and Leo call it."

Ted sighed. He knew Olivia was right to be frustrated. Boys and girls were not treated equally, and they should be. "Okay then, let's give Rachel the chance to go along," said Ted.

Echo had heard enough. He knew about the "Sure Enough Mountain Man" trip. Uncle Leo called it a rite of passage. Echo wasn't' sure what that meant, but that's what Leo had called it. A rite of passage. Even if he didn't know exactly what it was, the last thing Echo wanted was brainy Rachel tagging along on his rite of passage. That would sure give Buster Brasher something to crow about. Proving yourself meant doing it *alone*, not with your big sister.

As it turned out, Rachel was lying in bed listening to this conversation too. They both jumped from bed and skidded into the kitchen at the same time.

In a way that only a brother and sister could, Echo yelled, "I don't want her to go along," and Rachel shouted, "I don't want to go along." They looked at each other and smiled. It was almost like seeing bookends. Although Echo was two years younger and a boy, he and Rachel looked remarkably similar. Each had dirty-blonde hair, blue eyes, and a round face, like their father's. But that's where the similarities ended. Rachel was intense, wicked smart, and always willing to tell you exactly what she thought about any subject, especially when it came to the environment. Echo was smart too, but he carried it in a different way, mostly avoiding heated arguments and only inserting his knowledge when he thought it was needed.

In fact, his reluctance to tell you his own thoughts earned him the nickname "Echo." When he was a little boy, just learning to talk, he simply repeated everyone around him. If his mom said, "Time for supper," Echo would come out with, "Time for tupper." Or if his dad said, "It's cold outside," Echo would repeat, "It cold out-tide." Even as he got older, Echo would often repeat what someone said and then add his own thought to it.

One time when Echo was five or six, his Uncle Leo said, "This rain is tapering off. I think the fish will be biting tonight." Echo excitedly stood up and repeated, "This rain is tapering off, I think the fish will be biting tonight," then nervously added, "I'm going to go get my fishing rod." The whole room burst out laughing, and Echo's face turned red, until his uncle broke the awkwardness by saying, "Hmm, I think there's a little echo in here." And that was it. From then on, Theodore Orion, III was known as Echo. He had never been fond of being called Theodore, Ted, and certainly not Teddy, so Echo was alright with him. It also kept him from being confused with his dad and grandfather, who were both named Ted.

Now, Echo and Rachel, still smiling at each other, said in unison, "At least we agree on that!"

Olivia was the first to speak up. "Echo, I think I can guess why you don't want your sister going along, but Rachel, I'm curious about your reluctance. You love the woods."

"Well," said Rachel. "I've been meaning to talk with you and Dad about this. I heard you guys mention that the Sure Enough Mountain Man trip would happen in October and there's a science camp and special workshop on climate change that month and I really want to go." Before her mom could respond, Rachel blurted, "Billy Tyson is going too." This made Echo and even his dad snicker out loud. Billy Tyson was the son of a science professor and thought himself to be the smartest kid in Rachel's class. It was also common knowledge that Rachel had a brontosaurus-sized crush on him.

"That's enough, you two!" said Olivia. "Rachel, honey, let's talk about your science camp later. Right now your brother has some explaining to do about having to be rescued by Luna Woapalanne last night."

Echo grabbed a glass of orange juice and flopped into a chair at the kitchen table, where his parents were seated. His dad started to speak, but Echo cut him off. "I know, I know. It's not that big of a deal. I'll tell you what happened." Ted grimaced at his son's impolite behavior, but bit his tongue and let Echo go on.

"I stopped at the edge of Chestnut Flats and had an apple, then walked toward the rhododendron thicket where I'd seen Z-Buck go in the past. Not too far inside the thicket, I jumped a big deer and thought that it might be Z, so I started following him best I could." At this point, Echo's dad began nodding as if he knew what happened next.

Echo paused, and his mom said, "What is it, Ted?"

"Nothing really," Echo's dad said. "I just know how easy it is to lose your bearings when tracking an animal . . . especially when every rhododendron shrub looks just like the last one."

"Exactly!" Echo exclaimed. "Before I knew it, everything looked the same and I had no idea which way was home.

I walked for a long time toward where I thought Mud Lick Road should be, but there was nothing but more of that stinking rhododendron. It got dark, and the batteries in my flashlight were weak, so I was stumbling and starting to panic. I think I was walking in circles, and the sky was gray, so there were no stars for me to navigate by. I knew that Venus should be shining in the west, but I just couldn't see her. Snow began falling, and I started to freak."

Echo's mom broke in. "I should have never let you go up there so close to dark, and you, young man, were not prepared."

"I know, mom, but let me finish and you'll see that I did the right thing. I forced myself to stop and think, 'What are you supposed to do when you are truly lost?' *Don't move. Someone will find you. Start a fire to stay warm and signal searchers.* So I stopped and built a fire with torn up bits of my homework and strips of rhododendron bark."

"Oh, dear lord, Echo. Please tell me you didn't burn your math homework. You're barely passing that class," blurted Olivia Orion.

"Don't worry, Mom. Mr. Kepler likes me. He'll let me do makeup work."

Echo continued to unfold his tale. "When the snow began falling, I could see that it was not coming straight down, but at an angle, and hitting all the trees on the same side. I remembered that our snowstorms mostly come from the west, so the sides of the trees catching the snow must be facing roughly west. I knew I had to walk southeast to get home, but before I could get started, I heard a dog. Not a regular dog, but an angry dog, snarling and baying like it had an animal cornered. The hair on my neck stood up, and all I could think of was the pack of wild huskies that killed poor Curly in *The Call of the Wild.*"

Rachel had been eavesdropping and poked her head around the corner with a baffled look and asked, "Weren't you scared?"

"Yes!" said Echo. "By this point, my flashlight was deader than Curly, so I wrapped one of gym socks on the end of a stick and lit it on fire like a caveman torch. I crouched, pointing the torch toward the dog sounds, and waited with the little homework fire flickering at my back."

"Then what happened?" demanded Rachel, who was secretly intrigued by her brother's story but trying to act like she could care less about some silly search for a stupid deer antler.

"It was strange," said Echo. "All went quiet except for the occasional whistle of an Eastern Screech Owl somewhere behind me. I didn't think much of it until I realized the owl was getting closer. I spun around with the torch thrust out in front of me and nearly caught Luna Woapalanne on fire. She had crept up right behind me. How she got there without even popping a twig is beyond me. She looked like the Wicked Witch of the West in the torchlight, and I yelled for her to stay back while I waved the torch in wild circles."

"I would have fainted," said Rachel. "At school we call her old Loony Luna. That woman is maximum creepy!"

Ted Orion laughed out loud. "Luna is harmless, and I think you kids should get to know her better. She could teach you a lot."

"I'd like to teach her a thing or two about the importance of soap!" replied Echo.

"Okay, you three. Let's wrap this up. I've got to finish breakfast, and your dad has snow to shovel," said Olivia.

"Well, there's not that much more to tell. When I realized who she was, I calmed down and she backed away without a word. For a few seconds we just stared at each other. Then she asked who I was and if I was oaky. I told her I was Ted and Olivia Orion's son and that I got lost while looking for a shed deer antler. She just nodded real slow and said, 'Come on, let's git ya home.' She stomped out the fire and then grabbed an old open-sighted .22 rifle she had leaned against a tree. She pointed the gun's muzzle toward Mud Lick Road while giving me an angry stare. After a few steps in that direction, she whistled just like a screech owl and two big coonhounds came out of the night like smoke creeping along the ground. It was plain spooky.

"At the truck, I pulled the passenger door open and was hit with an awful stench—kinda like wet dog and old tuna sandwich! Looney Luna didn't seem to notice or care. I tried putting down the window, but it was stuck. The whole way home, I held my breath long, exhaled, then breathed in through my mouth. Luna just stared through the dirty windshield over the dusty layer of bird feathers, deer antlers, and bleached bones that littered the dashboard."

"Sounds a lot like your natural history collection," blurted Rachel. "Maybe, but I didn't care. I just wanted out of that stinky, rolling ecosystem of a truck!" Everyone laughed as Echo pretended to be choking from fumes.

Before anyone could scatter, Ted hollered, "Wait a second, Echo. We need to talk about this more later. I need to remind you about what it means to be prepared when you go in the woods. Your Sure Enough Mountain Man trip is coming up, and it seems you've got a lot to learn!"

The rest of the day was uneventful. Echo helped his dad shovel snow and thought about how much he didn't know about the woods. For as long as he could remember, he wanted to be a hunter and a Sure Enough Mountain Man, just like his dad and Uncle Leo. But he was shaken after getting lost on Chestnut Flats. Maybe he wasn't cut out for the

tough, survival stuff. Maybe he should stick to natural history. As he crawled into bed that night, something was bothering him . . . What did his dad mean when he said, "You kids could learn a lot from Luna Woapalanne"? *What could we possible learn from a gray-haired old woman who dresses like a man and smells like a bad tuna sandwich?* As his mind turned on the question, his eyes fell shut and sleep came.

5

SKINNY CHIPMUNKS

Thursday, October 14th

10:09 a.m.

Echo sat with his back against the big white pine's craggy trunk, his badly swollen right foot heaped with cool, wet leaves. As his mind emerged from the fog of concussion, his nerve endings reminded him of his other injury. The left side of his face stung, and his neck, just below the bone of his jaw, throbbed. Probing with the fingers of his right hand, he felt a brush burn and dried blood on his face. At his neck, his fingers found sticky blood, like chocolate syrup, and a puncture wound large enough to fit the tip of his index finger. Continuing the search with his hand, he squeezed the blood-soaked collar of his wool jacket and then noticed that his left sleeve was streaked with rivulets of crimson blood, like water running down a raincoat.

Echo peered around him now with the pain fully engulfing his neck and the beginnings of a fight or flight response growing inside. Adrenaline was snapping him into survival mode. His shattered two-way radio was still there, mocking him even from this new angle. But now he could see to the other side of the white pine where something else lay partially hidden in a few huckleberry bushes. As he fixed his gaze on the object, the first clear memories of the morning crushed him like a tidal wave. At once he felt sick again and dry-heaved from the bottom of his empty stomach. He knew now that he was in real trouble—not like forgot to do your homework trouble, but "OH CRAP, I MIGHT DIE TROUBLE!"

He had broken camp earlier that morning with a ferocious hunger consuming his every thought. Finding food on this Sure Enough Mountain Man trip had been much harder than he expected. This was a survival camping trip, and he only carried what he really needed. Heavy food was a luxury he couldn't afford. The plan was to supplement his supply of rice and oatmeal with wild edible plants, fish, and animals that he could trap or kill with his handmade bow. Echo's dad was strict about following hunting regulations, and since Echo wasn't yet old enough to have a hunting license, he was only permitted to take animals not covered by game laws. His dad had said, "Echo, the only exception to the hunting rule is if you find yourself in a true survival situation."

Following this rule, Echo became obsessed with hunting chipmunks, which weren't covered by the game laws. His first attempts failed miserably, but after dozens of tries, Echo became really good at creeping up on chipmunks and killing them with his bow. His breakthrough came after he learned a few tricks. First, if you can see a chipmunk's eyes, it can see you. Only move when a chipmunk's head is down or behind a tree. Second, if you get caught sneaking up on a chipmunk, act like you don't see it; look away and relax. Soon the little devils with their striped, camouflaged coats will relax too, and you can continue your stalk. On his first successful shot, Echo became so excited that he let out a whoop of joy and later smeared the chipmunk's still-warm blood in two lines on each side of his face.

It was near the end of a long day without food when Echo heard the *chup-chup-chup* call of a chipmunk coming from a fallen red oak tree. He moved from side to side, listening so he could triangulate on the chipmunk's exact location. By hearing a sound from more than one place, the human brain is pretty good at determining its location . . . but not as good as other predators. For example, Great-horned Owls have ear openings that are slightly offset so that they can find a mouse on the forest floor in complete darkness by sound alone. Then, they swoop in on silent wings for the kill. Once sure of his target, Echo belly-crawled, pushing the bow and one arrow ahead of him with his left hand.

At around twenty feet, he tripped the chipmunk's built-in predator detector, and it stretched out on the fallen oak log, allowing its stripes to do their work as natural camouflage. But it was too late. Echo had seen the chipmunk before it became one with the log. Rising to one knee, he drew the bow's string and shot in one fluid motion, toppling the chipmunk to the ground.

He skinned the tiny rodent and cooked its skinny body, "hot-dog style," on a green stick held next to a leaping fire.

Nothing ever tasted so good, and he went to sleep feeling like he'd just conquered the world.

But as the days went by, Echo learned that skinny chipmunks alone could not overcome his constant hunger and need for more energy. It seemed the simple act of living outside made the body burn calories twice as fast.

Hunger fueled carelessness, and it was this carelessness that landed him on his back with a broken ankle and a hole in his neck. No matter what angle he thought about it, Echo knew he was in deep trouble. To make matters worse, he seemed to be glued to the big white pine. He knew he should get up, get going, but he just couldn't summon the energy.

6

CHIEF BALD EAGLE

Sunday, January 17th

9:01 a.m.

It was Sunday morning, two days since Echo had been rescued by Luna on Chestnut Flats. He slept until the rays of a low winter sun streamed through his windows. He lifted the blind on the window nearest his bed and looked onto the glistening snow that covered everything. Cold air streamed in where the ill-fitting logs of the cabin met the frame of the window. On nights when temperatures dipped below zero, little fingers of ice would form on the inside of the window, near the leaky frame. Cold or not, the cabin was home, and Echo loved it there. Normally on a Sunday, he would race outside to work on some sort of project or just go adventuring in the woods. But this particular day he felt lazy. *Maybe I won't do much*, he thought.

A fuzzy particle of dust, illuminated by a shaft of sunlight, drifted through the air like a miniature parachutist and disappeared into the empty eye socket of an elk skull that was the centerpiece of Echo's natural history collection. Elk were now gone from most states east of the Mississippi River. Their populations had been destroyed by commercial hunting during the 1800s, before laws existed. Echo had read that the last elk in Pennsylvania was shot in 1877, not far from his house. But animals from Yellowstone National Park had been reintroduced to Pennsylvania in 1913, and now there was a growing population again. Every fall Echo's family made trips deep into the Pennsylvania Wilds to listen for the bugles of rutting bulls—a sound that tingled Echo's spine no matter how many times he heard it. And in spring, they scoured the forest for shed antlers. It was on a spring trip that Echo had found his prized bull elk skull with a large set of antlers still attached—likely the result of a mortal wound received during a fight with a larger bull. He remembered his excitement and pride as he cried for his family to come see his find.

Echo rolled from bed, sleepily walking to his collection. Without thinking, he looked into the eye socket of the elk skull as if expecting to see a tiny man with a brightly colored parachute, but there was nothing but dark. Feeling silly, he pulled his head back and rubbed his sleepy eyes. From this new perspective, he saw that his entire collection was very dusty, and an idea came to him. He thought, *I'll get a cup of hot chocolate, put on an audio book, and clean my natural history collection.* Although this might have seemed boring to other kids, he loved going through the "specimens" in his collection and recalling how he got them. There were cleaned skulls of birds and mammals, feathers, turtle shells, snake-skins, antlers, pressed leaves, fossils, cool-looking sticks, and tons of other treasures.

After a sip of hot chocolate, Echo dusted his opossum skull and counted the teeth to make sure all fifty were still there. Being more interested in animals than geography, he always remembered the number of states in the US by thinking of the opossum's teeth. He replaced the skull and picked up a stone arrowhead. This wasn't a reproduction like you find in touristy gift shops. Two years ago, he and his dad had found the head on the bank of Bald Eagle Creek when they were fishing for trout. Echo had dropped an imitation caddis fly that was made from deer hair. When he bent to pick it up, the arrowhead lay right between his feet, washed clean from a recent rain.

It was one of Echo's favorite specimens, and he would roll it in his hands, thinking about the Native American person who made it. What were they shooting at? Did they kill it? Were they starving? What was their bow and arrow like? Where did they live? He had so many questions about how people lived when they didn't have houses, electricity, or grocery stores. Just then, Echo was startled by a loud rap on his bedroom door.

"Teddy, can I come in? I've got something to tell you," his dad hollered through the closed door. Echo hated it when most people called him Teddy, but with his dad, it brought warm memories of when he was really little and his dad would come home from work and scoop up his little "Teddy Bear." Being named after your dad was sometimes hard. If people called him "Ted," he could be confused with his dad, but "Teddy" made him feel like a little kid, and he didn't want to be thought of as a little kid. When kids at school called him Teddy, it felt mocking, and he'd get a queasy feeling in his stomach—somewhere between being mad and embarrassed.

"Come on in, dad, but keep it down," Echo said. "I'm trying to be a zoologist in here." His dad came through the door laughing, and Echo cracked up too at the ridiculous idea that he was some famous zoologist, sitting in his little bedroom discovering a new trait about opossum teeth! Sarcasm ran wild in the Orion household. Ted Orion sat on the edge of the bed, looking nervous—a characteristic that wasn't typical for him. "Are you okay?" Echo asked. "Something tells me I'm not going to like what you have to say."

Echo's dad cleared his throat and began. "Do you remember what I said about Luna Woapalanne being able to teach you a lot?"

Echo cut his dad off. "Oh no. I don't want anything to do with that crazy lady."

"Just hear me out, Teddy," said his dad. "I'm going to tell you a little of Luna's story, and if you don't like what you hear, you don't have to visit her today after lunch like I arranged."

"What? You made plans with her and didn't ask me first?" cried Echo. "That's not fair and—"

His dad cut in midsentence with a firmer tone. "I know you and I know Luna, and I can't believe I haven't thought of connecting you two sooner. Please just listen to what I have to say.

"When your mom and I first got married, we intended to live off the grid so to speak—grow and hunt our own food, and sort of leave society behind. It was a dream . . . or maybe not a dream, but a crazy idea that didn't entirely work out. We bought a little chunk of timber near the state forest that had a rundown shack on it. It wasn't much more than a big tool shed with a woodstove for heat. We dipped our water from a spring out back, made light with kerosene lamps, and cooked right on the woodstove."

"Sounds awesome," Echo interjected. "Why did you leave?"

"Life had to move on, Teddy, but I'll tell you all about that another day," said his dad. "Let's get back to Luna.

Shortly after we moved into the 'Mouse Motel,' that's what your mom called the shack because it had so many mice living it—we had a visitor. I was splitting firewood one day when a tall woman simply appeared only ten feet from me—like she'd popped out of the ground or something. It was Luna. She awkwardly introduced herself, and that night we found ourselves having dinner with her and her father. It turns out, they lived in a hand-hewn log cabin right in the state forest, about a half mile from the Mouse Motel."

"Dad, why haven't you ever told us any of this before?" asked Echo.

"Well, Teddy, it's somewhat of a sad story, but I think you're old enough to hear it now. Luna was born in that cabin and has lived there her whole life."

Echo cut in again. "You mentioned her father, but where was Luna's mother?"

"That's one of the story's sad and confusing parts," replied Echo's dad. "Just let me tell you the whole story, and then you can ask questions, Teddy." Echo fidgeted on the edge of his bed, but was intent on listening.

"Luna's mother was from a family who claimed to be direct descendants of the famous Native American chief named Woapalanne. In his tribal Lenape language, Woapalanne meant Bald Eagle, so Whites referred to him as

Chief Bald Eagle. Most local people today believe that Bald Eagle Creek, Bald Eagle Mountain, Bald Eagle Valley, and so forth got their names from the bird, but it was really from the mighty Chief Bald Eagle and his band of warriors.

"Wait a minute," said Echo. "Does that mean my school—Bald Eagle School—was named after Chief Woapalanne?"

"I guess that's true," said his dad. "In fact, the town of Milesburg, where your friend Buster Brasher lives, was once called Bald Eagle's Nest. It was the place where Chief Woapalanne planned his bloody war parties."

"What war parties? Who was he fighting?" Echo demanded.

"It was during the American Revolutionary War in the late 1700s, and he was fighting to keep his tribe's land by attacking White settlements that were popping up along the West Branch of the Susquehanna River. Woapalanne's raiders would sneak into the settlements at night, killing as many Whites as they could in bloody hand-to-hand battles. But the chief's violent ways caught up with him, and he was brutally killed by the frontiersman and notorious Indian fighter, Sam Brady, in revenge for killing Sam's brother, James."

"What happened after the chief was gone?" Echo asked.

"Well," said Echo's dad, "it was a terribly difficult time for Native Americans. Thousands died from a disease pandemic not all that different from today's coronavirus, and the chief's remaining Lenape people were forced to flee their native lands for areas that were unsettled by Whites."

"So if they all died or fled to someplace else and Luna was born here, how can she be related to Chief Woapalanne?" asked Echo.

"Things weren't so simple. Some of the surviving Lenape remained behind and married Whites, creating mixed-race families like Luna's. But many people wrongly thought of the Indians only as savages who shouldn't be accepted into society. For generations, these Native American ancestors and mixed-race people hid their identities to protect their families."

"Wow, that explains a lot," Echo said.

"What do you mean by that?" asked Echo's dad.

"Well, Luna seems more than crazy. She seems mean and mad, like you'd be if someone took from you what didn't belong to them—like your best pocketknife. But do you think Luna is really related to Chief Woapalanne? That seems like a stretch."

"Well, that's a good question, Teddy, and unfortunately we may never know with so many people gone and family names being all mixed up. You see, on the bitter-cold, moon-lit night when Luna was born in that cabin, Luna made it, but her mother didn't. She died giving birth to Luna. Luna was raised by her father and has been looking for answers her whole life. She only knows the secondhand stories that her mother passed to her father and her father passed to her. There's a rumor that she has some sort of secret book, like a family tree that links her to Chief Bald Eagle, but most don't believe that it's true."

Ooh, this is getting interesting, thought Echo.

Suddenly, a loud voice rang down the hallway. It was Rachel, reminding Dad that she needed a lift to Science Club and they needed to get going.

7

A HUNGRY FOOL

Thursday, October 14th

10:17 a.m.

Still sitting against the big white pine, Echo craned his neck to peer again at the object partially hidden in the huckleberry brush. He could see the dappled black, brown, and rust of the wing. The outstretched pinkish-gray foot . . . and even the crest of the dead Ruffed Grouse. A few feet away lay the broken shaft of his arrow with a shiny smear of blood along its length. He sighed in disgust with his foolishness and childish lack of restraint. As if to torture himself, he couldn't stop thinking about all the mistakes that led up to the very bad situation in which he now found himself.

About an hour after breaking camp earlier that morning, Echo neared an unusual place where two small streams, one from the east and another from the west, flowed into Young Woman's Creek. This three-way intersection of water courses looked like the three forward toes of a turkey's foot. As he wondered if this was the spot he'd found on the map, a burst of thunder erupted near his feet. The sound startled him, but he recovered in time to see the Ruffed Grouse land in a big white pine twenty yards ahead. This was a gamebird, covered by game laws, and off-limits to Echo and his bow. But the gnawing hunger obsessed him, and his mouth watered at the thought of roast grouse, hot from the fire and dripping with juice.

At first he thought, *I'll just get close enough and see if I can draw my bow without being detected.* Getting within bow range proved easy, and he understood now why some people called the Ruffed Grouse a "fool hen." Grouse have evolved two strategies to avoid predators. Using their short, rounded wings connected to powerful breast muscles, they burst from cover and fly like feathered rockets to evade immediate danger. Their other strategy is to remain stone-still, allowing their mottled feathers to act as camouflage to hide in plain sight. Echo's grouse had used both of these strategies, but since he had seen the grouse land, the bird's strategy of hiding in plain sight wasn't working so well.

Echo shuffled his feet into shooting position, raised his bow arm, and drew the string until the middle finger of his right hand settled into the corner of his mouth. Adjusting his bow arm upward, his arrow's shaft and the grouse came into the same sight picture. And then it happened! Without Echo making a conscious decision, the arrow was off . . . like it had a mind of its own. "NO! I didn't mean that," roared Echo. But it was too late to take it back. The arrow hit its mark, and in a puff of feathers, the bird was struck dead, tumbling only a couple of feet before being caught up in a tangle of branches thirty feet above the ground.

Echo was hit hard with a jumble of confusing feelings. Pride, grief, and guilt all washed over him at the same time. He'd heard his dad talk about hunter's paradox, which is the strange brew of emotions hunters get immediately after killing an animal. But this was different. Not only did Echo kill a living creature, but he'd done it illegally—and worse, it was stuck in the tree where it would go to waste.

Thoughts raced through Echo's mind like machine-gun fire. *Should I walk away and never tell anyone? I'm in the wilderness; no one would know. Maybe I could throw sticks or rocks to knock the grouse from the tree. No, that probably won't work . . . too high and too many lower branches to get a stick through.* Then, a terrifying thought came to Echo's mind. *I could climb the tree and scoot onto the outer branches where the grouse is tangled and knock the bird loose.* This frightened Echo, as he knew the branches of white pine were flimsy, especially near their ends. Butterflies filled his stomach, as he *knew* deep down what he had to do. Hunger, guilt, and his profound respect for wildlife would not let him walk away.

He moved to the tree, leaned his bow against it, and threw his backpack to the side. The few lower limbs that he could reach were broken off and nothing more than stubs that he could get a toehold on. As he climbed, longer, thicker branches jutted from the trunk, and he went up easily until he was about thirty feet up and on the same level with the grouse. He made the mistake of looking down and immediately became panicked. A cold sweat formed under his collar, and for what seemed like forever, he was frozen, unable to force his hands or feet in any direction.

He remembered a trip to an amusement park with his family. He was on one of those merry-go-rounds where you have to catch the brass ring while balancing on a moving wooden horse going in circles. He was afraid to reach for the ring until his dad said, "Forget about the horse. Just focus on the ring until it's time to snag it." That's what he had to do now. Focus on the grouse until it was time to snag it. With renewed concentration, he crawled away from the tree's trunk and onto the middle portion of the limbs, which began slowly sagging under his weight. He found that if he inched slowly, he could counter the sag and ride it out, like staying up on a floating log.

With just three feet to go, he knew he'd never make it. The limbs were bending too much and would soon snap or dump him to the ground like a load of wet snow. He reached left to snap a dead branch that he could use to dislodge the grouse . . . AND THAT'S WHEN IT HAPPENED!

His shifting center of gravity was too much. He tumbled over like a tower of Jenga blocks and then dropped like an apple from Newton's tree. Not straight down, but like a rag doll bouncing from limb to limb, with bigger branches catching him hard on the head and neck. He was unconscious before hitting the ground with a sickening thud.

8

KINDRED SPIRITS

Sunday, January 17th

1:15 p.m.

In the truck on the way to Science Club, Rachel told Echo and their dad about how air bubbles got trapped in ice that froze millions of years ago, and if you analyze the bubbles from an ice core, you can tell what the Earth's atmosphere was like at the time. She said in an even, but authoritative tone, "Do you know that our atmosphere now has more carbon in it than at any time during the past 650,000 years and that more carbon means warmer temperatures?"

"I like it warmer," said Echo.

"Oh, no you don't," snapped Rachel. "Warmer weather means melting polar ice, which causes sea levels to rise and pushes salt water up our rivers. Salty river water kills fish and spoils our drinking water supply."

"Okay, so how do we get rid of all that carbon?" asked Echo.

"It's really hard," said Rachel. "Today in Science Club we are going to talk about something called Natural Solutions. It's a way to trap carbon in trees and soil."

"We're here," Dad announced as they pulled into the school parking lot.

When his dad returned to the truck after walking Rachel inside, he said, "Okay, Echo. Are you ready to go visit Luna?"

"Do I have to?" asked Echo, knowing the answer would be yes.

"Just keep an open mind," said his dad.

They rode in silence as the roads grew smaller and smaller, eventually turning to dirt. Echo loved taking rides through the state forest and peered out the window looking for birds, deer, or any other wildlife he might spot. Abruptly, his dad stopped the truck at a two-track road leading into the forest. He said, "Let's take a walk." In a few minutes, they were standing in front of a wood-sided shack with a tin roof.

Echo noticed that his dad was wearing a giant grin. "What is this place?" asked Echo.

Smirking, his dad said, "Why, it's the Mouse Motel!"

Excited, Echo said, "Can we go in?"

"It looks abandoned," said his dad. "I don't see why not."

There were just two rooms: a small kitchen area and a larger room with a wood stove. The walls were lined with hooks fashioned from pieces of deer antler and shelves made from small logs split in two to make a flat side. A mouse scurried across the floor. Echo's dad yelled, "There goes one of the motel customers!" Echo burst out laughing. Through the dust and spider webs, Echo saw something sticking out from behind one of the shelves and yanked on it.

He gasped with surprise. It was an old picture of his parents sitting close together on a freshly chopped log in front of the Mouse Motel. Olivia Orion was making a silly kissing face and wore a red handkerchief on her head and a T-shirt that said *Tom Petty Live 2004*. His dad was shirtless, with brown hair to his shoulders, one arm around Echo's mom and the other holding an axe above his head.

Echo's dad laughed and said, "Gosh, I remember that like it was yesterday," and then pointed to a log bench by the wood stove. "That's the log we were sitting on in this photo. Your mom and I turned it into a bench."

Echo walked over and sat on the log bench, running his hand along its cut end and feeling the axe scars with his fingers. He was deep in thought when his dad said, "Let's go, Echo. We're going to be late."

Back in the truck, Echo couldn't take his eyes off the photo and wished there was some way he could have known his parents back then. To see them living off the land would have been something.

In a few minutes, they pulled onto another two-track road and then up to one of the coolest cabins Echo had ever seen. It looked just like the settlers cabins he had seen in movies, with wide white chinking between the hewn logs, a front porch with a sloping roof and mismatched floorboards, and a stone chimney on one end that was broad at the bottom and narrow at the top. White smoke curled from the chimney's opening, disappearing into the cold blue sky but leaving behind the sweet scent of burning oak. A giant set of white-tailed deer antlers was tacked above the door.

A distinct shiver ran down Echo's spine; not a bad shiver, but one that told him something about this scene was triggering his deepest emotions.

In comparison to the neat cabin, the outside was strewn with old trucks and random piles of firewood. A pair of coon dogs sleeping on the porch suddenly leaped up and began barking in drawn-out howls with their noses tipped to the sky. The heavy wooden cabin door opened silently on leather hinges and a harsh woman's voice yelled out, "Boone! Crocket! Quiet down, you lazy dogs!" Echo shivered again, but this time the feeling wasn't so pleasant, and he wondered for at least the twentieth time why his dad was bringing him here!

Luna turned to Echo and his dad. "Well, come on in, it's cold out," she said. The inside of the cabin smelled of baked bread, fresh-cut wood, and some type of solvent . . . maybe gun oil, like the Hoppe's Number 9 stuff that his Uncle Leo used. At first, it appeared the cabin was a chaotic mess, but it didn't take Echo long to see the pattern. This was a place where things happened. There was a .30-30 Model 94 Winchester rifle in pieces on the kitchen table, a sawhorse contraption stood in the living room with curls of some yellowish wood underneath it, and by the woodstove was a straight-backed hickory chair and a small table piled with scraps of leather, flakes of shiny rock, and recently knapped stone arrowheads. The shiver was back, and this time it was good again.

Without any sort of socially accepted greeting, Luna simply said, "Your dad tells me they call you Echo. Is that right?"

"Yes ma'am," Echo replied.

"No need to call me ma'am. Do I look like a ma'am to you? Luna will do," replied the old woman.

Luna looked the same as she did the night she rescued Echo from Chestnut Flats—long gray hair below her shoulders and her tall, angular body inside a pair of men's work overalls. Luna started for a door off the living room and then turned back to Echo. "No calling me Looney Luna behind my back either. You kids think I don't know what you say about an old woman." Echo felt his face go red. He started to say something, but Luna flashed a look that said, "Better just drop it."

She opened the door and motioned for Echo and his dad to follow. Echo's mouth fell wide open when he saw what the room held. The walls were lined with jaw-dropping artifacts—a red wool blanket with primitive figures of elk and hunters stitched in black; longbows and arrows carved from wood; quivers made from coyote and even skunk hides; tomahawks with stone heads; flintlock rifles with powder horns hanging from the trigger guards; a skinning knife; steel animal traps; and a headdress filled with Bald Eagle feathers. While there was too much to take in, one object stood out and was clearly valued above the rest. Alone on the back wall hung a tattered deerskin jacket with its back facing into the room. On it was a large Native American symbol. It was like nothing Echo had ever seen, and he couldn't take his eyes from it.

Luna's voice, now softer than before, broke Echo's trance. "The walls have things from my Lenape heritage and from a life of living in the woods. These wooden cases hold my natural history collection." Echo thought he'd faint looking at the perfectly preserved and displayed animal skulls, feathers, bird eggs, furs, pressed leaves, and rows and rows of stone arrowheads. Then there was an object that put a lump in Echo's throat—a shed deer antler with its longest tine shaped like a letter *Z*.

Echo was just about to jump in with a million questions about the antler and everything else when Luna snapped her head toward the kitchen. "Oh crap, the bread!" she yelled in her gruff voice, cupping a hand over her mouth as if to apologize for swearing. Echo chuckled to himself as they followed Luna back to the kitchen, where she pulled two loaves of bread from an antique wood-fired cook stove.

After shoving the Winchester parts to one side of the table, she motioned for Echo and his dad to sit on rickety oak chairs. She put a thick slice of buttered, homemade bread and a cup of black coffee in front of each of them.

"I don't really drink coffee," Echo protested softly.

"You do today," said the old woman. "It goes perfectly with my bread."

The bread was the best Echo had ever eaten—crunchy on the outside and soft on the inside, with salty butter to help it slide down. The coffee was bitter and left a bad aftertaste in Echo's mouth, but he drank it anyway, while eyeing his dad for a reaction. After patiently waiting to ask his question, Echo nervously said, "Luna, may I ask where you got that antler with the Z-shaped tine?"

The old woman stopped chewing and looked squarely at Echo. He thought he saw the hint of a smile cross her face. "I found it on Chestnut Flats the same night I found you huddled around that homework fire," said Luna. "It's just an antler. Do you want it?" she added without emotion.

"YES!" Echo blurted, which drew a harsh look from his dad. "I mean, yes please," Echo said in a calmer voice.

After they finished eating, Luna retrieved the antler from her collection and brought it to Echo, who was still at the kitchen table. He'd been waiting two years to get his hands on another of Z-Buck's antlers, and he ran his fingers over the tines and looked carefully at the shredded tree bark still stuck in the dimples at the antler's base. He looked up in time to see his dad wink at Luna.

On the drive home, Echo held the antler and the photo of his parents in his lap and wished he could have asked Luna all of his questions. His feelings toward her seemed to be changing from disgust to fascination. Maybe she could teach him a lot, and he certainly had plenty to learn before his Sure Enough Mountain Man trip.

9

THE GOOD GROUSE

Thursday, October 14th

10:31 a.m.

One thing was for certain. Echo knew he had to take action. He couldn't just sit against this white pine, pitying himself over a broken ankle, ringing head, and bloody neck. He needed to gather his thoughts and get motivated. He thought about what he'd learned from books on wilderness survival and from stories about real people who had managed to survive horrendous conditions. He couldn't stop thinking about Brian Robeson from the book *Hatchet*, which was a about a boy who survived alone in the wilderness after a plane crash. He realized Brian's story was fiction, but *Hatchet* was one of his favorite books, and he knew it by heart. "What did Brian do to get going?" Echo asked himself.

50

After recovering his senses from the plane crash, Brian made a plan and took stock of what he had to survive—tools, clothes, food, stuff like that. *But what was the other thing that got Brian motivated?* Echo thought, trying to remember. Something about faith in himself, but that wasn't exactly it. What was it? Then it came to him. It was what Brian's English teacher, Mr. Perpich, used to tell him. "You are the best thing you have." And Echo knew it was true. He had good teachers. He had great skills. He only needed to quit sulking and summon his courage to get moving.

With great effort, Echo rose up on his good leg and began hopping around. As he came across his scattered gear from the fall, he tossed it into a pile for later. Right now he had a more important mission: he needed a crutch if he was going to move any distance.

Echo found a stout stick about four feet long with a *Y* at one end. He wedged the first twelve inches of the straight end in the crotch of a tree and pulled until the stick snapped. This left a three-foot section with a *Y* at the top and a twelve-inch straight piece. Near his backpack, he found his belt knife and carved two notches in the straight piece that were the same distance apart as the prongs of the *Y*. He fit the notches over the prongs and lashed the straight piece to the prongs with nylon parachute cord from his camping kit. Next, he found a stick shaped like an *L* and split the long leg along its length to make a flat side. Then he made a flat surface on the long *Y* stick. With the flats sides laid together, he lashed the *L* stick to the long *Y* stick. Now he had a crutch to fit under his armpit with a handle that faced away from his body.

He stuffed his gear, including the broken two-way radio and dead grouse, into his backpack and grabbed his bow. His next thoughts were crystal clear and in this order: Shelter.

Water. Fire. Food. That's what he'd been taught. That was how you survived. The human body needed shelter for protection from the elements, and it was best to build that shelter while you still had strength. Water was next in importance. Even with proper shelter, a person can only survive for three days without water. Fire was third, as it provided warmth, and a way to sterilize water and cook. Strangely, food was the last thing the human body really needed. But it was among the first things to drive a desperate person insane. He'd learned you can survive for three weeks without food, but after just twenty-four hours, the ache of hunger becomes relentless. It consumes the mind.

People in extreme survival situations had been known to eat rancid food and even their leather boots to drive away the hunger-fueled insanity. Food was everything in the natural world too. Plants, called primary producers, made energy from the sun. Herbivores ate the plants and predators ate the herbivores as part of a complicated food web. At the moment, Echo was no different than a starving deer. He was simply a strand in the food web. His strand would either break or survive. That was up to him.

The mere thought of food brought a pang—no, a *tsunami*—of hunger to Echo's hollow stomach. Saliva filled his mouth and he spat it onto the forest floor. He *had* to eat before moving on. He pulled the grouse from his pack and laid it aside. Next he found two rocks about the size of small shoe boxes and laid them eight inches apart. Then he hobbled to the big white pine to find tinder and kindling. He broke dry, dead branches from the tree's trunk and found a spot where the tree was oozing pine pitch. He sliced the tarry pine pitch from the tree with his knife and dropped the messy glob into a handful of dry pine needles.

Back at the rocks, he sorted his fire-starting material into three piles—first, a chewing gum sized wad of pitch mashed up with the dry pine needles; second, paper-thin curled wood shavings that he whittled from the dry pine branches; and last, dry sticks the size and length of new number two pencils. To make a bed for the fire, he scattered some dry pine needles between the rocks.

Next, he placed three pencil sticks side by side on top of the pine needles and then added another layer of pencils on top running ninety degrees to the first layer. Echo made sure to leave plenty of air space among the sticks. He then dropped the pine pitch and needle mixture on top of the sticks and fluffed some more dry needles around it.

By this time, Echo's energy was gone, sapped by injury, fatigue, and intense hunger. His fingers trembled. Starting fires was tricky. It was easy to screw up and waste your energy. And Echo had none to spare. He took a minute to lean against his backpack and inspect his "fire lay." He wished for some dry grass and birch bark to make a nest for the spark from his flint and steel, but he had no energy to search for it.

He withdrew the leather "possibles bag" from his pack and took out a hunk of flint and a steel striker. Echo made several sharp, glancing blows against the flint with the striker, sending a shower of weak sparks onto the gooey pitch and dry needles. After several attempts, nothing happened. Not even a tendril of smoke. Anger boiled up in Echo. Through clenched teeth, he half screamed, half growled at the sky in open rage. "Why am I here?" he yelled to no one.

He wanted to be a hunter. He wanted to be a Sure Enough Mountain Man. He wanted to make his dad and Uncle Leo proud, but maybe he wasn't cut out for this. Maybe he didn't have the grit for the backwoods. He felt a lump in his throat. These were cowardly thoughts of self-pity, and he beat them back like a grass fire. "You are the best thing you have" Echo reminded himself. "Don't let the best thing you have go bad."

He looked over his fire lay again. It was too dense. He had a butane lighter and a bag of cotton balls laced with Vaseline in his backpack. He could start the fire in a flash if he wanted to. But his dad had taught him that there was honor in doing things the hard way. He couldn't give up yet.

He scooped up some of the dry needles and fluffed them into a loose ball, placing smaller pieces of pitch in the center. This time a strong spark from the flint and steel took. A small ember glowed, and Echo lowered his head to puff air on the fragile ember. The pitch jumped to life, bringing the needles to a ball of flame. He added some wood curls, and to Echo's delight, soon the fire was snapping. He topped the flames with a few of the larger sticks and sat back. The feeling was indescribable, like he was a caveman in east Africa discovering fire for the first time. He felt intense gratification. The irony was not lost on him. The white pine that had nearly killed him was now giving him fire, which in the wild was the same as life.

He added still larger sticks and then struggled to his good foot with the crutch under his right arm. He returned with a green striped maple stem about two feet long. Next, Echo cut the head, feet, and wings from the grouse and plucked the body clean of feathers. He shocked himself with his next move. Echo put the grouse to his face and ripped a bite of raw breast meat from the carcass with his bare teeth. The purple meat tasted okay but was rubbery, and he choked it down with disgust at his impatience. He ran the maple stick longwise through the body just below the backbone and suspended it, breast side down, over the bed of hot coals.

In just a few minutes, it sizzled and dripped with juice. He again tore out a hunk of breast meat with his teeth. Now it was succulent with a pleasant texture. There was surprisingly little meat on a wild bird the size of a grouse, and Echo stripped it to its bones in only a few bites. His wild hunger had been tamed for now. It was time to move on. Time for shelter.

10

FAIR AND SQUARE

Saturday, January 23rd

11:00 a.m.

All week, Echo looked at the new addition to his natural history collection and just couldn't figure out why it didn't make him happy. He felt almost nothing when he looked at Z-Buck's shed antler sitting amid the others in his collection. It was a prize he'd wanted for years. Why wasn't he excited to have it? If he thought about it too hard, the feeling that spread across his chest was pure guilt. Not guilt from forgetting to take out the trash when his mom asked him to, but guilt from having something that didn't belong to you . . . something you didn't deserve. The satisfaction of collecting natural things, and even of hunting, was from the work that you put into it. The effort, the skill, the planning that it took to cleanly kill a deer, identify a new bird for your life list, or find an antler. That was real accomplishment. Luna had found Z-Buck's antler on Chestnut Flats and had given it to Echo. She deserved it fair and square. Not him.

After school on a Thursday afternoon, Echo found the courage to talk with his mom about his feelings. Olivia Orion listened intently and let Echo spill all of his emotions. Olivia believed in quietly empowering her kids and had clever ways of encouraging them to make good decisions. After Echo finished, she asked, "Would putting the antler in a drawer so you couldn't see it make you feel better?"

"No! It would make me feel worse," Echo replied without hesitation.

"Then, what would make you feel better?" she asked.

"Giving it back and finding my own," said Echo.

"Then there's your answer," said Olivia with a look of satisfaction.

"You're right," said Echo. "I'll give it to Dad to take back to Luna."

"Wait a second," said Olivia. "Don't you think it would mean more if you took it back yourself?"

"Maybe," was all Echo said before heading to his room.

Echo wasn't sure what to make of Luna now that he'd been to her cabin. He once heard his Uncle Leo say that Luna was a "few fries short of a Happy Meal," and he believed it after the ride home from Chestnut Flats in that stinky truck of hers. But no crazy person could have such a beautifully kept natural history collection. You had to be smart and read a lot of books for that. Then there was the hardness. The way she snapped at him for calling her "ma'am." But that wasn't exactly right either. He had seen Luna be soft when she talked of her Indian heritage and even kind when she served them fresh baked bread. He wasn't sure what to think about the Indian part either. Was she really related to Chief Bald Eagle like his dad had said, or was she just nutty from living in the woods too long? She seemed to be so many things all at once. Crazy, but smart. Rough, but kind. Indian, but not Indian. Backwoods, but intellectual.

Just then, Echo's sister Rachel popped her head through his open bedroom door. "Time for supper," she said. "Your favorite, venison burritos."

At eleven years old and growing fast, Echo was always hungry and wasted no time finding his place at the table. Echo dug right into his burrito and said what was on his mind. With sauce running down his chin and rich venison filling his watering mouth, he said, "Dad, I want to return the antler to Luna."

Ted Orion smiled as if he'd just won a trivia contest. "Okay, when do we go?"

"Aren't you going to ask why?" replied Echo.

"Your mom has already told me how you feel, and knowing you as well as I do, I'm not surprised. I'll swing by Luna's cabin on my way to work to arrange another visit for us."

"Why don't you just text her?" asked Rachel. Ted and Echo burst out laughing. "What's so funny?" snapped Rachel.

"Honey, Luna cooks on a wood-fired stove and doesn't even have an old-fashioned telephone, much less a cell phone," her dad said.

"It's so cool. I want to live that way!" declared Echo.

On Saturday morning, Echo found himself in the passenger seat of his dad's truck as it bounced to a stop in front of Luna's cabin. New snow had fallen, and he could see a well-worn trail from the front porch to what Echo thought was a little tool shed, or maybe an outhouse. Just then, the door of the shed flew open and white smoke billowed out. Luna staggered from the smoke, holding two objects the way you might carry sacks of onions. The door, pulled by a long rusty spring, slammed closed behind her, and the smoke was cut off. Echo's dad rushed over to take the objects from Luna, but she shrugged him off and motioned to the cabin with a gesture of her head.

In the confined space of the cabin, hickory smoke wafted from Luna's hair and brown chore coat, mixing with the greasy smell of the two cloth sacks that she hefted onto the kitchen counter with a thud. The combined odor caught Echo off guard, and his stomach lurched a little. The hickory smoke was pleasing and reminded Echo of fall when his dad lit the first fire of the season in their woodstove. The sickening greasy smell was familiar too, sort of like the road-killed raccoon he'd picked up last summer. He was relieved when Luna suggested they go into the next room so she could warm her hands by the woodstove.

She stretched her knobby, crooked fingers to catch the stove's heat, and Echo noticed the cuts and calluses on her hands. A life in the woods was honorable, but not easy. There was an awkward pause until Echo's dad nudged him into action. Echo nervously held out the antler. "I brought Z-Buck's shed antler back to you. You found it. It should be yours, not mine."

Luna looked first at the antler and then softly into Echo's eyes. She seemed to understand his thoughts. Her gaze was open and not crazy or mean like it had been that night on Chestnut Flats. She even smiled a little as she took the antler and placed it gently on a table. "Your dad tells me that you'll soon be old enough to hunt."

"Yes, ma'am . . . I mean Luna," Echo corrected himself before the old woman could respond.

"He also says you'll be spending a few nights in the woods alone as part of some mountain man something or other." Echo shot his dad a look and was pretty sure he saw him wink at Luna like he'd caught him doing before. Something was going on, and Echo wasn't sure he liked it.

"A boy headin' for his first huntin' season needs a good weapon, don't ya think?" asked the old woman.

Echo's dad fidgeted and said, "I think you and Luna have some work to do. I'll be back to pick you up in a couple of hours." Before Echo could object, Luna was guiding him to a storage closet and Ted Orion was firing up his pickup truck.

When Luna pulled the closet door open, Echo was surprised to see a neat row of long wooden stakes leaning against the back wall. They looked like skinny, six-foot-long pieces of firewood that had been split from logs. Some were shaped like a piece of pie on the end and still had bark on the outside.

"These here are bow staves," the old woman said with a smile. "I've been cuttin' 'em 'round here for years." Echo had seen similar looking pieces of wood in a book on bow making that his dad had. Luna started pointing to individual staves. "This one is pignut hickory; hard as river rock but makes a good bow if you know how to work it. Right here in the middle, this bright yellow one is osage orange, one of the best bow woods, but they only grow down in the valley so I don't get very many. And this white one is white ash. It's easy to work, but is gettin' terrible hard to find since that freeloadin' emerald ash borer bug invaded from Asia and killed all the ash trees."

Luna turned to Echo with a serious look and said, "Hold out your hands, child." Echo instinctively thrust his hands forward, and Luna frowned. "Work side up," thundered the old woman. "I can't tell nothin' by lookin' at the purty side."

Echo was confused again. The old woman had gone from being kind to gruff in a heartbeat, and he didn't know what to make of it. He stuffed his feelings down and turned his hands palm side up. Echo squirmed and felt his neck flush with blood as the old woman grabbed his fingers in her rough, knobby hands. "Humph," Luna grunted. "Better than I thought. Strong lines, curved fingers, and some meat in those palms. You're a true hunter and a tough kid . . . or you will be." She pulled the pignut hickory stave from the closet and stood it next to Echo as if she was measuring his height. *A true hunter and a tough kid.* The words tumbled through Echo's brain and he beamed. A hunter maybe, but no one had ever called Echo a "tough kid." The words made him feel good inside.

Carrying the hickory stave, Luna walked toward the saw-horse contraption that sat in the living room near the wood stove. "This is a bow horse," the old woman said. "You use it to work a stave down into a bow. Sit down here and clamp the stave down by putting your foot on that pedal underneath."

Echo's feelings had been bubbling all morning, and the cork finally popped. "What's this all about?" he demanded. "Why am I here? And why are you and my dad always winking at each other like you're cooking something up behind my back?" Echo regretted the harsh words as soon as they left his mouth. He knew better than to talk to an adult that way, and he still didn't trust the old woman. Old as she was, there seemed to be plenty of spark behind those brown, wrinkled eyes, and he didn't want to cross her.

In an even tone that told Echo nothing of the old woman's mood, she said, "Let's have some lunch, child. I can see you're hungry."

Echo didn't know how anyone could see that someone else was hungry, but he followed Luna to the kitchen anyway. He was again walloped with the peculiar, road-kill smell from earlier. She motioned to one of the oak chairs, and Echo sat without a word. She poured a cup of thick, black coffee from an old-fashioned percolator pot that had been bubbling on the cook stove. The bitter taste was easier to tolerate this time, and he sipped lightly at the steaming coffee. Next, Luna slid a wood plank onto the table and then abruptly dumped the contents from one of the cloth bags on top of it. Echo recoiled and gasped with disgust at the sight. As he pushed back from the table, the back legs of his chair caught in a gap of the plank floor and he flipped over backwards with his feet sticking straight into the air like an overturned box turtle!

Luna tossed her head back and roared with laughter. "What's a matter, child? You never eaten smoked raccoon before?"

11

GIMME SHELTER

Thursday, October 14th

12:22 p.m.

Echo stuffed the Ruffed Grouse's severed wings into the top of his backpack and gently placed the bird's skeleton and other inedible parts onto the dying fire. He understood the seriousness of killing an animal and had been taught to be grateful for every life taken. Echo closed his eyes and gave silent thanks to the bird for giving its life so that his own life could continue.

Energy in the form of calories moved up the food chain through death. One thing had to die to pass its energy onto another. Echo knew firsthand that nature was often far more cruel than humans could ever imagine.

When he was nine, his family went to Yellowstone National Park on vacation. From a high bluff, they watched a pack of gray wolves hunting along the Yellowstone River. The powerful predators effortlessly took down a cow moose and her calf, first ripping the calf to ribbons as its mother frantically bellowed in distress. Then the bloodthirsty pack encircled the cow, taking turns lunging at her legs with bone-crushing bites. Soon, they pulled the cow to the bank of the river and began eating the guts from her belly before she was even dead.

Knowing that Ted Orion was a wildlife biologist, a person in their group begged him to do something, anything to stop the torture. But Ted said they should look away if they couldn't deal with reality. He said, "Nature isn't a movie. You can't just skip over the parts you don't like."

But just because killing was the way of things in nature didn't mean that hunters could take the act for granted. Echo's dad said that humans had the ability to "think," and that by changing just one letter in the word "think," you got the word "thank." He said, "If you can THINK, then you have a responsibility to THANK the animal that gave its life to you."

Eating the grouse before leaving the area of the big white pine had been the right choice. The warm meat had given Echo confidence and cleared his head. Using his crutch, Echo scraped moist dirt onto the hot coals and covered them with rocks to keep the fire from spreading. Watching the embers die out, he considered his options.

Echo's mom and dad were expecting him to arrive at their meeting place in about thirty-six hours, but it was miles away, with two steep ridges in between. He knew that he'd never make it on his injured foot. His parents, or whomever was coming to rescue him, would have to find him where he was. But there was a problem. A BIG problem. Echo hadn't exactly stayed on the path that he and his dad had agreed upon. He hadn't stuck with the plan and was in an entirely different creek drainage . . . miles from where he should have been.

Despite his promise to Luna that he wouldn't stray from his Sure Enough Mountain Man route to look without her, Echo had taken a detour to search for something. Something amazing. Something that would change what people said about Luna behind her back. Something that would make his family see that he was more than just a boy. Something that had the power to change history and right wrongs. They agreed to wait until they could search together, but Echo hadn't waited. It was too late now; none of that mattered at the moment. He had made bad decisions, decisions that put him in a real wilderness survival situation. The only thing he could afford to think about now was how he could survive until someone found him. To save his own life, he needed shelter: a place to be warm and heal his broken body.

Echo glanced up. Heavy clouds were clumping in the sky like bunched layers of dirty sheep's wool. He tried to re-member the technical name. Nimbostratus came to mind, but he wasn't sure. The temperature was in the low forties and would be falling overnight, so the coming storm might only bring rain. But here in the mountains, it could just as easily be wet snow. "Could this get any freaking worse?" Echo screamed out loud. He was at once startled by the raspy sound of his own voice. He didn't sound like himself any-more. The voice was his, alright. But not his old kid's voice. It was a new, deeper voice. Something had changed. Echo could feel it.

He shouldered his pack and began hobbling toward Young Woman's Creek, his hickory bow cradled in the palm of his left hand and the crutch working under his right arm. After some meandering, he circled back to the place where the three water courses converged to make the shape of a turkey foot. Two streams coming together to form a confluence was common. But three was something rare. He became more convinced than ever that this place, where three streams ran together, was the spot he and Luna had talked about— "the place of rocks where the spirit of the crow and the elk flow together with the young woman." He wanted to take a look at the map he and Luna had drawn, but there was no time for that now. He needed shelter.

Ahead, he could see a giant gray rock the size and shape of a pickup truck. An idea came, and he headed for it. Nearing the rock, he could see a second large rock lying next to the first one. The two rocks created an open space between them, like a hallway about six feet wide and as long as a pickup truck. He sighed with relief as his idea took shape. All he needed to do was fasten his oil cloth tarp over the top for a roof, then seal off the ends of the "hallway" and he would have rain-tight shelter.

Getting the roof in place was his highest priority. The problem was his injured leg. With two good legs, he would have scaled the rocks to pull the tarp in place, but he could not climb one-legged. In fact, after falling from the white pine, the very idea of climbing made his stomach twist. There had to be another way.

He laid the tarp out next to one of the rocks and removed a hank of parachute cord from his pack. The solution came fast as lightning, and he smiled inside at how good he was becoming at wilderness problem-solving. Echo uncoiled the paracord, tying one end to the tarp's center grommet with a bowline knot, which he could tie with his eyes closed. He tied the other end of the paracord to a stout twelve-inch stick and threw it up and over both rocks to the other side. The stick took the paracord with it. He limped to where the stick landed and pulled on the paracord until the tarp was centered over the gap between the rocks. Bingo! He had a roof. Using more bowline knots, he tied each of the tarp's four corners to nearby trees. The tarp was now tight and pitched downward at each corner to shed water or snow. Next he needed to seal the ends of his shelter.

Using oak poles and cross members that he cut with his hatchet, Echo made a ladder-like structure that he leaned against the rocks at one end of the "hallway." In the space between the ladder and the rocks, he layered sticks, brush, and hemlock boughs. To finish it off, he gathered sphagnum moss from near the creek to fill the smallest cracks. Now, one end of the shelter was sealed off from airflow. He did something similar on the other end of the gap, but left one side of the ladder loose so he could pivot it like a door. *Home sweet home*, he thought.

He looked at his Batman watch and got a funny feeling inside. Part of him was still a little boy, fascinated by little boy stuff. But a bigger part was almost a man, a Mountain Man capable of living anywhere on his own.

He'd spent two hours building his shelter and had three hours left until the night would turn his world dark. Now he needed to lay in firewood and get water. He had an intense urge to eat again, but that would have to wait. He could make it through the night if he was warm and had water to sip.

He remembered something his Uncle Leo had taught him: "Firewood is up, not down, you clown." It was a way to remember that dry wood was usually off the ground where it was exposed to air and not on the forest floor where it was saturated with water. By breaking and sawing dead branches from trees, Echo soon had enough wood for the night. Next, he headed to Young Woman's Creek with a thirty-two-ounce, wide-mouthed plastic Nalgene bottle and a thirty-two-ounce stainless steel bottle. It was good practice to make sure one of your water bottles was suited for boiling water over a fire in case you were caught in the woods without a pot.

As Echo knelt by the creek with his head down, he was hit with a sudden urge to look behind him. People who spent time in the woods, especially in dangerous situations, often felt paranoid when they were in vulnerable positions, like being hunched over for a drink from a noisy creek.

Rabbits and other prey animals had their eyes positioned on the sides of their head so they could detect predators in a nearly 360-degree arc around them . . . kind of like having eyes in the back of your head. Humans, on the other hand, were predators, and like most predators, had eyes on the front of the head. This gave good depth perception for attacking prey, but was a major disadvantage if you had a mountain lion creeping up on your backside.

Echo snapped his head around but saw nothing. He sat quietly, just listening, then filled the first bottle. Midway through the second bottle, he heard a faint swishing sound directly behind him and turned in time to pick up flash of movement. No detail, just the perception of movement. "Probably just a Blue Jay checking me out," he nervously told himself.

On the way back to his shelter, Echo grabbed handfuls of eastern hemlock needles—the flat oval ones that were dark green on top and whitish underneath—to make a hot tea that would provide some nourishment and hopefully stave off his hunger until morning. He lit a fire inside the shelter and was happy to see the smoke draw up and out to one side of his tarp. After two cups of the warm tea, he was suddenly exhausted. He laid out his sleeping pad and bag within reach of his firewood stack so that he could feed the fire throughout the night. His foot throbbed, and his neck oozed bloody puss, but he was safe and warm for now. His thoughts closed off and he dropped into a hard sleep, like the body does when it needs to repair itself.

12

BOOK ONE

Saturday, January 23rd

3:30 p.m.

At the sound of Echo and his chair hitting the plank floor, Boone and Crocket were on him, sniffing his hair and licking his face with their big coon dog tongues. This brought even louder laughter from Luna, and soon Echo was laughing too, big full laughs . . . the kind that make you snort through your nose. It seemed that even the dogs were laughing!

With a giant smile that Echo had never seen before, Luna came around the table and helped him right his chair. Immediately the smoked raccoon was back in his face, making his nose crinkle with disgust. "Just try it," Luna said. "If you don't like it, you don't have to eat it." The old woman worked some meat from the raccoon's bones and put it on a plate alongside a mound of homemade applesauce. She topped the meat with a spoonful of huckleberry preserves, made from berries she'd picked in the state forest. The raccoon was smoky and salty, like ham, but with a musky flavor. Echo liked it—a lot—and in a few forkfuls, he had emptied his plate.

Still smiling, and now with a sort of grandmotherly look, Luna added more raccoon to Echo's plate and cleared her throat to speak. "I'm sorry if I haven't been open with you, child," Luna said. "Your dad told me about your Sure Enough Mountain Man trip, and it sounds an awful lot like the vision quest that my ancestors practiced for thousands of years. It was a custom for our Lenape boys, and sometimes girls, to mark the time when they were no longer children by going into the forest to dream. If they were lucky, a guardian spirit in the form of a fox, a hawk, or even an ant might find them. This spirit would protect them for life and make sure they never forgot the lessons they learned from being alone in the woods."

The old woman sighed before continuing in a nervous way that Echo did not expect. "I thought maybe I could help you with your own vision quest, or whatever you want to call it. You see, ever since my father died a few years ago, I don't have anyone to look after. He was a true mountain man, tough as turtle hide, and he taught me everything I know about living in the woods. But when he got old and sick, I had to take care of him—dress him, feed him, and dig a hole when . . ." Her words trailed off and she quickly looked away, wiping the corners of her eyes with those knobby fingers.

There was a long silence before Echo spoke. He was only eleven. Knowing how to deal with someone's grief wasn't something he was used to. "You must be sad," he finally said.

There was more silence. Then, thinking she might want to talk about her dad, he asked. "How did your father know so much about living in the woods, anyway?"

Luna turned toward Echo, smiling, but with a trace of tears still in her eyes. She slid a plate-sized piece of raspberry pie in front of him before sitting at the head of the table in one of the creaky oak chairs. "My father wasn't from around here," she said. "He grew up in Alaska, a far tougher place than our mountains. Make one mistake there and you're just as likely to die as live. Misjudge the ice on a frozen river, dead. Misread a momma grizzly bear's intentions, dead. Mistake an oncoming blizzard for harmless rain clouds, dead. You get the idea. Without a heap of woods sense, Alaska will chew you up and spit you out like a watermelon seed."

Luna continued, in a less somber tone than before, "My father's people were bush pilots. They lived in an Inuit village and flew government biologists and even big-game hunters all over the North Slope in little one-engine planes called Pipers. When he was just a teenager, only a little older than you, my dad was involved in a plane crash. He survived alone for thirty-three days by killing a caribou for meat and wrapping himself in its bloody skin to keep from freezing to death. From then on, he was highly respected by the local Inuit tribes. They gave him the name 'Bou,' which he kept for life."

"That sounds really scary," said Echo. "How did your father end up here in Pennsylvania?"

With this question, Luna's eyes became lively and eager. "Flying was a new thing in the 1930s, and the Piper airplane company needed experienced pilots to test their planes, so they brought my father to their factory in Pennsylvania. That's where he met my mother, sweeping floors on the assembly line." Luna's eyes suddenly brightened, like an idea had come to her old mind. She abruptly rose from her creaky chair and walked out, leaving Echo alone at the kitchen table with his empty pie plate.

There it is, he thought. The old woman had finally mentioned her mother. Echo's stomach tightened with nerves, remembering what his dad had told him. Did Luna's mother really die right here in this cabin, giving birth to Luna? That seemed more than a little creepy. Was the old woman's mother actually the great-great-granddaughter of the bloody Chief Bald Eagle, who ransacked White villages and famously murdered an army officer? And what about the rumor? Did Luna have some sort of secret book that told about what happened to the Lenape people? Echo got a sick feeling, wondering what the old woman was up to. Trust was building between the two, but it wasn't there yet . . . at least not for him. He heard the sound of her boots approaching on the plank floor and straightened in his chair.

Luna replaced Echo's pie plate with a tattered, leather-bound book. Crude letters, burned into the elk-skin cover, read, "Book One: Lenape Ways." "You seem like a smart boy," Luna said. "I need someone smart who I can trust to help answer some questions before they put my stubborn butt in the ground. My mother left me this book. It tells the Lenape history until the time when my people had to flee after Chief Bald Eagle was killed. Do you know who Chief Bald Eagle is?" the old woman asked.

"Yes," Echo answered without hesitation.

"Then why do you look so danged clueless?" Luna asked in a gruff voice.

"I thought your mother died when you were born," Echo asked uneasily.

Luna smiled. "Yes, that is confusing I suppose. My mother did die. I never knew her. She died giving birth to me . . . right over there in the next room . . . on the floor . . . wrapped in a wool blanket. She had no time to prepare anything. No chance to tell me my own history or hers. My father knew where she kept this secret book hidden and gave it to me when I was old enough."

Echo turned the book over and his eyes widened with recognition. On the back cover was the same symbol he had seen on the deerskin jacket hanging in Luna's natural history room. He ran his fingers over it and looked toward the room. "Yes," Luna said. "It's the same one."

The symbol was of a snapping turtle's back, with a bow and arrow superimposed over the shell, so the arrow's triangular-shaped stone point formed the turtle's outstretched head and the fletching made up the tail. "What's in it?" Echo muttered in a soft voice.

"It tells of our ways. Our spiritual beliefs. Our birch bark houses and hickory bows. What we ate and what animals we worshiped. How we hunted and trapped. It tells of the slaughter and enslavement of our people by the Whites. It tells the story of how the Lenape were eventually forced to flee west from their homeland on the Atlantic Coast to the frontier of Pennsylvania, but the writing stops in 1780. Just one year after Chief Bald Eagle was killed." Echo started to ask a question, but the old woman held up her hand to stop him.

"There's more," she said. "In the back is a handwritten note that seems to have been written after the book was done. It says there is another book. A second book that is hidden somewhere in the forest. This other book tells what became of our people after 1780. Where they went to hide and who they married. It has a family tree, showing the descendants of Chief Bald Eagle. All this was kept hidden to keep the names of the Indians who were war spies secret and, later, to protect the children of Indians who married Whites."

Excitedly, Echo asked, "Have you ever looked for book two?"

"Yes," replied Luna. "But there is only a single clue to finding a small book in all of Pennsylvania's woods."

"What is it? What is it?" blurted Echo.

"I will tell you, but it is useless," Luna said. "I have tried since I was a girl to find the answer." The old woman cleared her throat and read slowly, word for word, from the handwritten note. "Follow the turtle north in the place of rocks where the spirit of the crow and the elk flow together with the young woman."

Just then, Boone and Crockett began barking from the front porch. "Your dad is here to pick you up," Luna said. "Please keep this a secret, Echo. I need your help, but I don't need everyone in the county knowing about this. They already think I'm just a crazy old lady."

"You have my word," said Echo.

"Here, put this in your pocket and see what you can discover, my smart boy." Luna handed Echo a scrap of paper with the clue written on it.

Echo winked at her and said, "See you next weekend for some bow building."

13

THIN RED LINE

Friday, October 15th

6:56 a.m.

Only sooty gray light seeped into Echo's dim rock shelter as he awoke from his hard sleep. There were no details, just gray walls and weak shafts of light, like a dungeon. In his half sleep, Echo got that panicky feeling that comes with waking up in a strange place. He sat bolt upright, spinning his head this way and that to get his bearings. *Where the hell am I?* he thought. It took Echo a full minute to mentally connect the dots that had led him to this point.

His mind flashed through the details like an old movie projector. "I was on my Sure Enough Mountain Man trip. I foolishly left the trail to look for Luna's book. I fell from a tree and broke my ankle. I can barely walk and need to be rescued."

How would anyone find him in this remote creek bottom, two miles from his planned route? His dad's words kept ringing in his ears: "Stick to the plan, and if anything goes wrong, I'll be able to find you. If you don't stay near the trail, it'll be like finding a needle in a haystack."

Stupid, stupid, stupid! was all Echo could think to himself as he lay in his sleeping bag. "I'm a stupid needle in a stupid haystack!" But Echo's survival training didn't allow him to wallow in his negative thoughts for long. To stay positive was to survive. That he knew.

Echo shivered inside his sleeping bag. It seemed much colder than he thought it should be. This was his sixth morning in the woods, so he was used to the nippy night air. But this was different. *A biting cold. A dangerous cold*, he thought. Echo remembered reading about Ernest Shackleton's expedition to reach the South Pole in 1915. His team became stranded on an ice floe for months. The constant wind made their eyes water, causing tears to freeze into icicles on the ends of their noses. Each time an icicle was broken off, it took a chunk of frostbitten flesh with it. Echo squirmed at the thought and knew he needed to get busy.

With a stick, he scraped at the coals of his fire and was happy to see a few tiny orange embers hiding beneath the ash. He had laid aside some dry grasses for just this purpose. He put a fluffed ball of grass on the coals and leaned small sticks against it to make a teepee. With a few puffs of breath on the reluctant coals, he had a neat little fire dancing off the rock walls.

He was fully awake now and something was gnawing at him . . . like when he knew his mom had asked him to do something but he couldn't remember what it was. He looked around to make sure his stuff was there. Backpack, check.

Bow with quiver and arrows, check. Hatchet, check. Even his crutch was there, check. What was he forgetting? He glanced up. Tarp for a roof, check . . . But wait a second. Why was the tarp sagging like a pig's belly?

"Oh no," he gasped, suddenly remembering the gathering storm clouds he'd seen the day before. Echo crawled to the shelter entrance and peered out. White! Everything was white. At least four inches of wet snow coated the ground and clung to the trees, and it was still coming down in big, wet, ugly flakes.

The snow would delay his rescue, perhaps for days. A quick stab of worry hit Echo straight in the gut, then the feeling was gone as quick as it had come. Normally this sort of setback would have knocked the wind from his sails, but that was the old Echo. He had changed, and he knew it. The time spent alone relying only on himself had toughened him, had built confidence where insecurity used to live. He felt different too. He guessed he wasn't quite a man yet, at least not like his dad or Uncle Leo, but he sure as heck wasn't the same kid who walked into the woods six days ago. "I can figure this out on my own," he said aloud in a sturdy, calm voice. "I am my best asset."

Echo grabbed his field journal and started a list of the day's most important things:

1) Wrap my ankle with something.
2) Put out some signals for rescuers to see.
3) Lay in more firewood.
4) Find food.
5) Boil more water from the creek.

He thought of adding "Look for Luna's book" to the list, but that was ridiculous. He had to forget about the book; no time for that anymore. He didn't even know if that silly book existed . . . or if Luna's stories were even true. This last thought made him feel guilty. The old woman had no one to lean on. No one to believe in her. At least he could be her friend. She should be able to trust him.

His ankle was feeling a bit better, but was still far too swollen to fit inside a boot. He cut an extra T-shirt into strips and wrapped his foot to immobilize the joint. He stretched a wool sock over the wrapping and then cut a waterproof booty from a bright orange rain poncho. He held the booty to his foot and sealed the seams with several wraps of duct tape from his kit. "Not bad," he thought. "At least my tootsies will be warm and dry." He cut the rest of the poncho into long strips, then finished getting dressed.

Outside, he tied the orange poncho strips to trees on all sides of the shelter so rescuers could see them from any direction they approached. Now he turned his attention to firewood. The snow covered any wood that might be on the ground, but he didn't care about that anyway. The best firewood was dry branches still connected to trees. It was slow going, but he had the crutch thing figured out and could now move short distances before having to rest.

After two hours, he figured he had enough pine and hemlock wood to keep his little fire going for at least a couple of days if he didn't burn it too hard. All the while, the sky continued to dump slushy snow. It was time to warm up and dry out. Before returning to the shelter, he found a stick about ten feet long and dragged it through the shelter entrance, being careful not to upset his fire.

Using his hatchet, he cut the stick just a little longer than the distance between the rock walls inside his shelter. He wedged the stick between the rocks about five feet above the ground, so that its own tension held it in place . . . kind of like a shower curtain rod. He stripped out of his wet outer clothes and draped them over the stick to dry. His foot was throbbing from the exertion of getting firewood, and he desperately needed to eat. He laid out the sum total of his food on top of his backpack: one packet of instant oatmeal, a strip of venison jerky, and a half-eaten Snickers candy bar.

Nearly twenty-four hours had passed since Echo had eaten the grouse, and before that he'd only had a skinny chipmunk here and there. He needed big, full calories. He wanted a greasy bacon, egg, and cheese sandwich, but the oatmeal would have to do. He relished every sweet bite and scraped the cooking pot clean with the spoon of black cherry wood that he had made especially for this trip. Echo was nowhere close to satisfied, but maybe the oatmeal would "stick to his ribs" long enough to take the edge off. He smiled a little at the thought. His Uncle Leo was always saying stuff like that. "Here, eat this, it'll stick to your ribs and make you grow strong."

Echo's beech calendar stick was lying next to him, and he carved a sixth ring in it. For six days he had woken up in the woods and not in a cushy bed surrounded by walls. He wondered how many more rings he'd carve before getting to sink his teeth into a juicy cheeseburger.

Just then, something crashed behind him, and Echo wheeled defensively with his camp knife thrust out, as if a bear had just blown through the back door. He was relieved to see that only his drying rod had fallen, dumping his heavy, wet clothes to the ground. While replacing the rod, Echo noticed that its fall had knocked a large chunk of Sphagnum Moss from the rock wall. He was noticing how he could fit the moss back onto the rock like a piece from a jigsaw puzzle when something on the rock face caught his eye. Straight lines weren't common in nature, yet there it was—a straight, thin line, running side to side in a faded red color.

With the pliers of his multi-tool, Echo began gently removing more moss from near the thin red line. With each pluck, the full thing—the full beauty of it—became more visible. He needed both hands now to steady his nerves as the weight of his discovery sunk in. Was this really it? Echo's blood coursed like a raging river by the time the image came into full view. Here it was at last—the clue that confirmed his suspicions were right. The clue that confirmed that Luna was not crazy at all! He knew now that the book should be close! He just needed the strength to find it.

14

SMARTS AND WAYS

Saturday, May 22nd

2:00 p.m.

Throughout spring, Echo visited Luna many times at her cabin. They marked the passage of time by the return of migratory birds from the south. The noisy Snow Geese had migrated through in long white "V" formations during March. April brought the return of the Eastern Phoebe that nested under Luna's porch roof. And now that it was May, Wood Thrush sang their flute-like songs by day, while Whip-poor-wills pierced the night by repeating their own name—*whip-poor-will—whip-poor-will*—until the sun cued the end of their shift.

Luna and Echo used their time at the cabin to work on the hickory bow that Echo would carry on his Sure Enough

Mountain Man trip. The bow would be one of Echo's most important pieces of survival gear, and Luna taught him step-by-step how to make a deadly wooden bow, powerful enough to kill even a bear. But it didn't end there. She also taught Echo many things about life in the woods. Things Luna had been taught by her father. With a laugh, Luna would say, "My daddy had a heap of backwoods bush smarts and not much else . . . Well, except for the strongest hands and biggest heart on the mountain. Child, you let me pass it on, and you'll have a heap of bush smarts too."

There was much more to Luna than bush smarts, though. She also taught Echo from the Lenape Book of Ways that was her mother's. "Get your head right, child," Luna would say as she geared up to teach Echo some new bit of wisdom. The old woman taught him how to track even the smallest animal, how to build deadfall and snare traps, and how to make a poultice from medicinal plants. Echo already knew a great deal about plants and animals from his dad and Uncle Leo, so it was Luna's lessons on the weather that he found most fascinating.

When the leaves of maples turn over to show their undersides, a storm of thunder and lightning will soon come.

When dew is on the grass in the morning, it will not rain during the day. When it is not there just after darkness, it will rain before morning.

When birds fly low and silently, a bad storm is coming.

When the dove sits close to the trunk of the tree during the daytime, a great wind will soon blow.

When the blackbirds flock together and start south when summer is still with us, there will be much snow during the winter.

When the muskrat builds a low house of reeds and mud, the winter will be mild, but the larger and higher the house he builds, the worse the winter will be. And when he builds no house at all, but instead burrows beneath the ground, prepare for severe cold, for the waters of swamps and ponds and smaller streams will freeze to the bottom.

There seemed to be no end to Luna's teachings, and Echo drank them up like cold root beer at a July baseball game.

Luna called her way of living "Smarts and Ways," as it was a perfect blend of hardcore bush smarts and the old ways of her Lenape ancestors. Echo liked learning "Smarts and Ways." Bush smarts were straightforward tactics that could get you through anything. The Mountain Men of the 1840s honed their bush smarts to trap beaver and survive the Rocky Mountain winters in expertly built log cabins. Having solid bush smarts took plenty of skill and physical ability, but not much else.

The Lenape ways were different. Living by the old ways was about letting the land tell you what to do. Letting it tell you how to live, how to survive within it without needing to overcome it. Luna always reminded Echo that bush smarts was about living *off* the land, while the old ways meant living *with* the land. The old ways taught of patience and a spiritual connection to nature. With a Mountain Man father and a Lenape mother, Luna seemed perfectly adapted to live in both worlds. Sometimes she told stories to teach Echo how to think about "Smarts and Ways."

One April day, as a deafening rain pounded on the cabin's tin roof, Luna said, "Child, stop scraping on that bow. This rain reminds me of a story that might just teach you something." Echo stopped his work and looked at the old woman who was hunched over, stitching a piece of deerskin for some project she seemed to be hiding from him. Luna sat up, wincing at the unexpected temperature of the cold coffee she just slurped from her cup, and then started in.

"After days of rain, a Mountain Man on his way to catch the buffalo migration comes to a flood-swollen river that he cannot cross. He uses his great skill during a day and night of hard work to build a log raft that will float him to the other side. He reaches the migrating buffalo herd on the second day, but is so tired he must sleep and does not wake until the buffalo are gone. An Indian comes to the same uncrossable river. With great patience, she builds a simple shelter, fishes, and rests for two full days while the water goes down. Then full of energy, she wades to the other side and reaches the migrating buffalo, only to see the last animal pass by. The Indian asks the Mountain Man, 'How many buffalo did you kill?' 'None,' replies the Mountain Man. 'I was too tired to hunt. How many did you get,' asks the Mountain Man of the Indian. 'None,' she replies. 'I rested too long at the river and the buffalo were gone.'"

After Luna finished, Echo sat quietly, trying to understand the significance of the story and expecting an explanation that did not come. The old woman silently turned back to her stitching without another word, and Echo went back to his bow, thinking of bush smarts, old ways, and buffalo not taken. *What does it all mean*, he silently asked himself.

That was weeks ago, and Echo was still trying to figure out what the story meant. Perhaps he'd get up the nerve to ask Luna today when he visited . . . that is if he ever got there. He was frustrated at having to tag along with his mom and dad to see his sister Rachel get an award for her science fair project. As they entered the school auditorium, Echo noticed

Rachel staring toward the stage where a panel of judges sat. In the middle was Billy Tyson, student president of the Science Club and the object of Rachel's affections. Echo elbowed Rachel in the ribs and made a kissy face at her. She snapped her head away, but not before he saw the color of a tomato bloom in her cheeks. He snickered to himself, but felt a little bad too. He was close with his big sister and didn't want to ruin her important day.

After a lot of boring announcements and prizes for the second and third place winners, it was finally Rachel's turn. Billy Tyson stepped up to the microphone to explain Rachel's project. Echo glanced at his sister, who was excitedly fanning her face with a paper copy of the awards program. He flashed her the thumbs-up, and she smiled nervously. Billy began, "Today's first place winner designed a brilliant science project that even I am envious of." Billy "the Brain" Tyson thought himself the smartest kid in the class and wasn't afraid to let everyone know how highly he regarded his own intelligence.

Billy went on, "Before I announce her name, let me tell you about her project. This young scientist downloaded atmospheric data from NASA's computers to develop a statistical model that predicts how much habitat certain species of wildlife will lose under various climate change scenarios. For example, she has predicted that the Wood Thrush, a Neotropical migratory bird, will lose more than fifty percent of its breeding habitat if the mean temperature rises by three degrees Celsius. Her predictions will help inform conservation actions for these great species. Please join me in congratulating Rachel Orion on her first-place science fair win."

Rachel was the center of attention and deserved every minute of it. Echo was very proud of her. There was a round of hearty applause and lots of chitchatting before they were finally on the road to Luna's place.

At the cabin, Boone and Crockett stood howling from the front porch, with strands of silvery drool dripping from their brown dog lips. "Yuck!" cried Rachel.

Echo laughed and shook his head. "They're actually quite loveable," he said to her jumping from the truck and waving goodbye to his parents and sister. As he crossed the porch, Echo patted Boone and Crockett on their heads and gave a quick knock on the cabin door before letting himself in.

Luna was in her chair working on the secret leather thing again and jumped up when Echo came into the room. "Oh, it's you, child," she said. "I thought those lazy dogs were finally gettin' after that big ole groundhog that's been diggin' under the porch. Sit." She pointed to a chair at the kitchen table. "I've got something to fill your belly."

Echo sat and noticed that his hickory bow and a block of beeswax were already on the table in front of him. "I'm hungry," he said, "but I might need a drink to wash down a bow and some beeswax." At first the old woman seemed confused, but then she got his wisecrack, and with a toothy grin said, "Shush, child, I'm getting your food." Echo laughed at his own joke and pulled the bow onto his lap to examine its lines. "Eat this," said the old woman. "It will fix your smart-aleck ways. After your snack, we'll get to work on your bow."

Knowing Luna's fine cooking, Echo readily bit into the toast that had a golden jam-like substance spread on the top. "Good Lord!" Echo hollered. "What is this? It's terrible!" He reflexively spit a half-chewed mouthful back onto his plate as the old woman broke into the loudest cackling laugh Echo had ever heard.

"Ramp preserves," cried Luna through her laughter. "Made 'em myself. Good medicine for a wiseacre like you!" Ramps grew wild in the forest and were sort of a cross between garlic and onions. "Two can play at your game," she said as she slid another piece of toast in front of Echo. "I think you'll find this one to your liking."

This piece was covered with the huckleberry preserves that Echo loved, and he ate it eagerly to wash the rotten ramp taste from his mouth. "C'mon, wolf that down, and grab your bow and that hunk of beeswax. We'll work outside," the old woman said.

While Echo etched the specs on his bow, Luna kindled a fire in the yard to melt the beeswax and blend it with some bear fat so that it could be rubbed into the bow's wood. On the bow's limb, just below the grip and facing toward the shooter, Echo wrote: *62" 44# @ 28."* This meant the bow was sixty-two inches long and had a draw weight of forty-four pounds when pulled to twenty-eight inches. Below the specs, in his best handwriting, Echo wrote, *Sure Enough Mountain Man, October 2021.* On the top limb, where he could see it when shooting, he etched, *Smarts + Ways.*

Luna handed Echo a jar with the warm beeswax concoction and he began rubbing generous portions into the bow with a soft linen cloth. In a few minutes, the grain of the wood was full and took on a shine, like the skin of a polished apple. When he was satisfied, he leaned the bow on the porch and returned to the fire with Luna, where they sat on rounds of firewood stood on end like stumps.

The two were silent for a while, just watching the fire and listening to an Eastern Towhee sing "drink your tea." Through the spring, they'd tried solving the handwritten clue left behind in the book that was Luna's mother's. But, as Luna had told Echo months before, it was no use. The code, or whatever it was, was impossible to break. The second book of ways would be lost forever. But now, Echo had new information.

Echo spoke in a quiet, almost apologetic voice to contain his own excitement in case what he had to say was a lot of nothing. "Luna, I didn't give up."

"What? Speak up, child. You know I can't hear," fumed Luna.

"I didn't give up," Echo repeated in a stronger voice.

"Give up what?" Luna asked with irritation in her voice.

"I didn't give up trying to solve the riddle about the second book of Lenape Ways. You know, 'Follow the turtle north in the place of rocks where the spirit of the crow and the elk flow together with the young woman.'"

"Yes, of course I know. Go on, child," said Luna.

Echo took a deep breath and started unloading what he had discovered. "Okay," he said. "Listen to this. From the first book of Lenape Ways, we know that after Chief Bald Eagle was killed in 1779, his raiding parties were broken up, leaving no one to protect the remaining tribe. A band of Lenape people, led by one of Chief Bald Eagle's daughters named Waving Grass, is said to have fled north to a remote wilderness to escape attacks by the White army."

"This is where things get fuzzy," Echo continued. "Near the end of the book it says that the band was traveling to a place near the west branch of the Susquehanna River where there were still large herds of elk."

"Yes, I know all this, child I've been over that book a thousand times," Luna said in exasperation.

Echo nearly cut her off in his excitement to get it all out, but bit his lip and let her finish before continuing. "Here's where it gets interesting. Using my iPad—"

"Using your *i* what?" grumbled the old woman.

"iPad," replied Echo. "It's a sort of computer that you use to surf the internet."

"What on earth does any of this have to do with surfing, child?" questioned Luna.

Frustrated that the old woman wasn't taking him seriously, Echo said, "Just listen and forget about all that other stuff. On the internet I found old maps from the 1800s that were posted by some historical society down in Harrisburg. They focus on rivers and creeks since those were used to float logs to sawmills. Get this; the maps also show the places where the surveyors saw the biggest herds of elk. This was important information back then because elk were still being hunted for money and people wanted to know where to find them. I noticed that one of the last large herds was in a mountainous area near what is now the town of Renovo. The map shows that the elk were common along a tributary to the river called—are you ready for this?—Young Woman's Creek!"

Luna was now connecting the dots, and Echo had her full attention.

Echo paused to let all of this sink in and then went on, "I zoomed in on the maps with my iPad and searched up and down Young Woman's Creek. You won't believe what I found, Luna."

The old woman leaned in. "Come on child, spit it out. What, pray tell, did you find?"

15

TRACKING TURTLES

Friday, October 15th

9:49 a.m.

Echo had seen pictures of famous cave paintings made by early human hunters in what is now France. What he saw on the rock wall of his shelter at this very moment didn't seem much different . . ..just better. *More artistic,* he thought. Echo went to his backpack and retrieved a small cardboard tube. From it, he pulled the sketch he'd made by copying the Lenape symbol from the back cover of Luna's book. He held the sketch next to the red cave painting and whispered, "Perfect match." It was a snapping turtle's back, with a bow and arrow superimposed over the shell, so the arrow's triangular-shaped stone point formed the turtle's outstretched head and the fletching made the tail.

The only difference was the way it faced. On Luna's book, the straight line of the arrow and its point faced upward. On Echo's shelter wall, the arrow pointed to the left, which Echo knew was north. His excitement grew as each new piece of the puzzle dropped into place. He glanced at the note he'd written beneath the sketch: *Follow the turtle north in the place of rocks where the spirit of the crow and the elk flow together with the young woman.* If he hadn't been in the tight space of a survival shelter and balancing on only one good foot, he would have jumped for joy!

The word "luck" kept coming to Echo's mind. He was dang lucky to have found "the place of rocks" and even luckier to have chosen these particular rocks for his shelter. What wasn't lucky was the condition of his enflamed foot and his hollow stomach that begged for even the tiniest morsel. He could follow the turtle north only after he'd rested his foot and filled his empty gut. He hobbled to the entrance of his shelter and scooped snow into his cooking pot. Back inside by the fire, he unwrapped his ankle and poured snow on his bare skin to reduce the swelling. After fifteen minutes, the pain eased and he re-wrapped the joint. He ran his fingers over the puncture wound in his neck, feeling the hard, sandpapery scab. It hurt, but didn't compare to the crippling effects of a lame foot.

Now he must tend to his hunger. With his bow and crutch, he slithered through the shelter's narrow entrance. Moving any distance to find food would be impossible. He needed another dose of luck if he was going to eat today. While the snow complicated his rescue, it at least made animal tracking possible. Echo knew that creeks running through the forest were like superhighways for most animals. Some species, like mink, even specialized on these riparian zones for building denning sites and searching for aquatic food, such as crayfish. Echo followed Young Woman's Creek, hoping to cut a track he could follow. He used a technique called "still hunting," which involved moving only twenty or thirty yards and then stopping for at least ten minutes to observe. He made sure to stop next to trees or shrubs that would break his human outline, allowing him to blend into his surroundings like a ghost with a bow.

At his third stopping place, Echo put his back to a large black gum tree and kept watch on a stand of Norway spruce trees directly in front of him. He'd been there what seemed like an hour and was about to move on when a red squirrel dashed across the snow from one tree to another, twenty yards away. The squirrel had clearly spotted Echo. It stopped on a branch just ten feet off the ground to scold him with its chattering call. This chatter also served to alert the entire forest to Echo's presence. Soon, Black-capped Chickadees, Tufted Titmice, and White-breasted Nuthatches were buzzing around him, calling loudly in a behavior called "mobbing." Echo smiled. He knew what was happening. While revealing their presence increased the chance that small animals could get eaten by a predator, that risk was offset by making sure all eyes and ears could track the intruder among them. This lessened the chance for a surprise attack.

Echo had nothing to lose, so he crept toward the noisy squirrel for a closer shot. But when he got too close, the squirrel felt threatened and zipped to the other side of the tree, where it continued chattering as if to say "Nana nana boo boo!" Echo knew how this game usually ended, but his growling tummy pushed him on. He must eat. He eased around to the squirrel's side of the tree, but the little devil simply swapped sides again, keeping the tree between itself and Echo. All the while, the birds gave agitated calls and dive-bombed Echo's head.

A trick his dad taught him came to mind. Echo draped his plaid wool jacket over a witch hazel bush and plopped his hat on top. Then he moved to the other side of the spruce tree. Now, as far as the squirrel was concerned, there were two Echos to keep an eye on. Not knowing which Echo was the real deal, the confused squirrel began jetting from one side of the tree to the other. Finally, it lingered too long on what was the real Echo's side. A quick instinctive shot with a stone-tipped dogwood shaft brought the chattering to a stop and the whole forest fell silent. Echo took a moment to let the gravity of death settle on his spirit and then gave a silent thanks for the exchange of life. He thought of Luna as he put the warm squirrel in his jacket pocket and turned for his shelter.

On the way back, he discovered a set of fresh tracks that crossed his own in the new snow. No, not just crossed his track, but actually had followed him, maybe even stalked him. The tracks appeared to belong to five or six coyotes, probably a family group. He suspected they'd approached and watched him play cat and mouse with the red squirrel before getting nervous and moving off. Now he wondered, who was the cat and who was the mouse?

With its hair, skin, and guts removed; Echo placed the red squirrel in a pot of water along with some wild onions he'd picked a few days earlier. Boiled tender, he ate the flesh and savored the hot, meaty broth. Simmering wild meat into a stew captured the animal's precious calories far better than roasting it over an open flame, which caused the vitamin-rich juices to drip away.

By now his parents would be panicked. Echo had not done his morning check-in by radio, so they were probably frantically keying the mic, trying to reach him on a two-way radio that was shattered to bits. His dad was most likely setting off to search for him at that very moment. Little did he know he would be searching two miles away, in the wrong place. Echo sighed and tried not to go down the rabbit hole of "what if I would have done this, or not done that . . ..or just stuck to the freaking plan." *Man up*, he thought. *Or better yet, Mountain Man up.* He was frustrated with himself, but he no longer felt scared. He knew the woods. He had "Smarts and Ways." He could do this thing.

Feeling the effects of the warm squirrel stew, Echo closed his eyes and dozed for a short while before sitting up with a violent start. He had dreamed that a young Lenape girl was holding his hand, pulling him through the forest while excitedly pointing to Lenape turtle symbols that seemed to be on every tree. She was leading him somewhere, but where? She was motioning for him to follow and mouthing words that he could not understand. The dream was fuzzy, and none of it made sense, but one thing was clear. He must follow the turtle symbol he found in his rock shelter. RIGHT NOW. "Get up!" he told himself.

He stared at the turtle on the wall, committing its every detail to memory. He even bent down and sighted along the northward-pointing arrow with his right eye. He couldn't see beyond the brush wall he'd built over the shelter's opening, but he struck a mental bearing to follow.

Outside, he stretched his arms like a weathervane and tried to align himself with the direction the turtle was pointing. He followed the fingers of his north-pointing hand and picked out a white oak tree some twenty yards away. He limped to the tree with the crutch working under his right arm. Now, he spread his arms again, one pointing back to the rock shelter and the other north. He was flabbergasted to see his finger pointed directly at a giant boulder thirty yards away. He moved to the big rock and began scraping the moss a way with his crutch . . . and there it was! About halfway up the rock face, like a red tattoo, the Lenape turtle was there pointing north. Dead ahead now was another rock, and Echo half ran to it, kicking up snow with his crutch as he stumbled along. A few scrapes with his crutch and there was the red turtle. Again, pointing straight ahead. Now he could see a line of three more boulders spaced about twenty yards apart.

His heart pounding in his ears, he went to the boulders. On the first, he found the turtle easily by knocking loose a few chunks of moss with his crutch. He staggered to the next boulder and again, with nothing more than a swipe from his crutch, he located the turtle symbol neatly applied in some sort of red pigment that had withstood more than a century of rain and snow. Emboldened now, he rushed toward the third and final boulder. But it was as if some great evil spirt reached a filthy hand from the ground and swept Echo's legs clean from beneath him. With no time to break the fall, his face slammed to the ground, sending wet snow up his nose and into his eyes. He rolled onto his back and saw that his crutch was sticking up from the forest floor like a fence post. It had become wedged between rocks, setting Echo up for an epic face-plant.

The fall sent a shockwave of blinding pain up Echo's leg, reminding him of just how dangerous his situation was. He was alone and injured with no food, and his search party was likely days away from finding him. He thought of the Mountain Man, Hugh Glass. In 1823, Glass was mauled by a momma grizzly bear and then abandoned for dead by his so-called friends. With a broken leg and maggot-infested wounds from the bear's razor-sharp claws, the unstoppable

Glass slithered like a snake on his belly for weeks. He lived on only roots he grubbed from the ground and low-growing berries that he could reach from his prone position. Eventually, he came to the Cheyenne River, where he built a crude raft and floated to safety. Glass had survived on pure will, and if Glass could do it, Echo reasoned, he could too. The will to live. The will to succeed. The will to be something bigger, to be something more than a boy. That sort of will was strong medicine indeed. *Screw the crutch*, Echo thought, and crawled like Glass the remaining distance to the last boulder that lay ahead.

16

MUSAK CREEK

Saturday, May 22nd

5:15 p.m.

Luna kicked at the fire nervously with the toe of her boot, making tiny sparks crackle and take to the air. From her seat on the round of firewood, she looked intently at Echo and repeated her request. "Get out with it, child. What did you learn about Young Woman's Creek from your old maps and fancy-pants iPad?"

The old woman was clearly mocking Echo, but he didn't care. *Just wait till you hear what I have to tell you*, he thought. Their friendship had grown deep over the months, and they were able to tease one another without worrying about upsetting each other. That was part of a true friendship.

"With my fancy-pants iPad," Echo said, "I found a spot on Young Woman's Creek where two smaller creeks flow in from opposite sides. They are named Lebo Creek and Shaney Creek. The three creeks make a really cool shape like a turkey's foot."

"That's odd, but so what? What do Lebo and Shaney have to do with our clue?" asked Luna.

"When I zoom in on the old maps, it shows me the original names of these little creeks before they changed."

"What do you mean?" the old woman asked.

"The railroad and logging companies stopped using the names the Indians gave the creeks and renamed them after different stuff, like important people."

"Okay, I follow you," said Luna with increasing impatience. "Just get it out. Tell me what you found, child. I've been waiting for this my whole life!"

"Well, Lebo Creek used to be called Three Crows Creek and Shaney Creek"—Echo looked at the old woman's face before going on, wanting to see her reaction"—was once called Musak Creek."

Luna turned ghost white and Echo raced to her side to prevent her from falling into the fire as she momentarily blacked out. After coming to, the old woman blinked hard, tears trickling down her cheeks and getting caught up in the deep wrinkles before reaching her chin. In a vulnerable voice, Luna asked, "Are you sure about this, child?"

For the first time, Echo realized how important it was for him to be right. Being wrong about this thing that had plagued his friend for so long would be cruel. Giving hope where none existed would be wrong. But he had to be right. He had looked it up on several websites. Musak meant elk in Lenape. This had to be it—*the place of rocks where the spirit of the crow and the elk flow together with the young woman.*

They both heard tires on gravel and turned to see Olivia Orion coming up the driveway. "Thank you! Thank you, child," Luna repeated. Echo reached out and tenderly squeezed Luna's bony, weathered hand. The gesture surprised both of them. Echo quickly pulled his hand back and smiled awkwardly at her. "We'll find it," he whispered. Echo trotted to the porch for his finished bow and then hopped in the truck with his mom.

Hi, honey. How was your day?" Echo hated it when his mom called him "honey." He was almost a man, for crying out loud. At least there was no one else around to hear it.

"Doing great, mom. What do you think of my bow?"

Olivia Orion was impressed. She had gone to college to be a teacher and had often thought of homeschooling Rachel and Echo, but she never seemed to have the courage. Even so, she asked lots of questions like teachers do. Thinking fast, Olivia asked, "Is that made from one piece of wood or two?"

Echo smiled inside. The boy in him still loved to show off for his parents, so he could see their excitement.

In an authoritative tone, he said, "It's a selfbow made of pignut hickory cut from Luna's woods."

"What makes it a . . . what did you call it . . . a selfbow?"

In response to his mom's question, Echo could really show off, and he launched into a full-blown archery lecture.

"Modern bows are called composite bows because they are made from many pieces of wood, and usually fiberglass too. They use glue to hold it all together. But a selfbow is made from just one single piece of wood. No glue. Isn't that amazing? Nothing else. Just wood, and it doesn't break. It's the same way the Indians made their bows. First you cut a tree down and remove a log about six feet long. Then you split the whole log from one end to the other, first in half, and then in half again and again until you have long sections that are shaped like pieces of pie on their ends. These are called staves, and each one makes a bow. You let the staves dry in the sun until they are ready."

"That sounds like a lot of work," remarked Olivia.

"It is, but it's fun too," said Echo. "It's like splitting really long pieces of firewood."

"Okay, what's next?" his mom asked.

"Luna gave me a hickory stave that she already dried. First, we scraped the bark off the wide side of the pie until it was clean white, like bone. But here's the tricky part. You have to find one of the tree's growth rings and follow it for the whole length of the stave. If you accidentally scrape through the growth ring, you have to start over and scrape down to the next growth ring to get a fresh start."

"Why is that?"

"Any break in a growth ring causes a weak spot where the bow will break when you pull it. It's like bending a piece of dry spaghetti that already has a crack in it. It will always break at the crack before it bends to its full potential."

"That makes sense," Olivia said.

Echo continued. "After that, we marked the outline of the bow on the stave with a pencil. I used a hatchet to cut along the pencil line, like using scissors to cut a Halloween ghost from a piece of paper."

"Only way more dangerous," his mother said with worry in her voice.

"Oh, Mom. It's fine. You just have to be careful and always chop away from your body."

"This is interesting. Keep going," Olivia said.

"After I had it cut to shape, we used the hatchet and sharp stone scrapers to thin the limbs so they would bend. I just kept scraping and scraping until I had a bow. I think it's the coolest thing I've ever done!"

His mom smiled. "What makes it so special to you?"

"I love the idea that I could take something from nature and turn it into a tool—a weapon—that I could use to survive and feed myself. It feels like I'm connected to the forest and could do anything with just my hands and brain."

"Wow, Echo, that's really deep. Tell me more. What else?"

Echo thought for a minute. "I think growth rings are pretty sick," he said.

Olivia smiled and shook her head. "Sick" was a slang term she could never figure out. How was being sick a good thing? But she didn't say anything. Echo continued without noticing his mom's bewilderment. "A tree adds a new growth ring each year. In good years, the rings are wide because the tree grew a lot. In bad years, like when there is a drought or forest fire, the rings are narrow. So, you can look at the rings and pick out the crappy years and then imagine what might have happened to the tree that year. Luna helped me to count back eleven rings to the year I was born—it was a very good year!"

Just then, Olivia began to brake as they pulled in the long driveway the led to their cabin. "Dad's home!" cried Echo. "I can't wait to show him my bow."

Ted Orion was impressed with Echo's selfbow and pulled his own recurve bow from the rack so that he and his son could practice shooting in the backyard.

17

BOULDER SHRINE

Friday, October 15th

12:53 p.m.

Without his crutch to use as a scraping tool, Echo used his bare hands to tear stubborn clumps of moss from the third and final boulder in the line he was following. The moss held jagged ice crystals from the night's bitter cold. It was like running your fingers over shards of frozen glass that were woven into a mossy blanket. Tiny, painful slits like paper cuts wept blood from Echo's fingertips, but still he kept at his task. Just like Hugh Glass, dragging his own tattered carcass, inch by inch, foot by foot, there was no stopping until the job was done.

He had risked his life by moving off the trail to search for the second Book of Lenape Ways, and if he survived, his parents would surely be disappointed—even angry—with his poor decision. If he could find the book, at least he'd have something to show for his mistake. He might even be a hero instead of just an irresponsible lost kid who needed to be rescued. No, there was no stopping now. Echo ignored the blood and kept clawing at the stubborn moss. Finally, there it was. Fainter than the rest, but no doubt a Lenape turtle symbol pointing north. But north to where? Unlike the past symbols that always pointed to another boulder, this one pointed to nothing but a forest of trees. He slumped against the boulder to think for a moment.

His hunger was back with a vengeance. Out here it never seemed to stop. His body was consuming itself to stay warm, to mend an injured foot, and just to stay alive. Living in the woods gave a person a whole new perspective on what it meant to simply have enough food. "There was never enough," Echo thought. He shoved his bloody, aching hands inside his shirt, against his bare skin to thaw. When his dexterity returned, he unzipped his pack and took a long drink of water, hoping it would beat back his insane craving for a Philly cheesesteak from his favorite sandwich shop.

Soon he realized something strange. He couldn't actually see very far in the direction the turtle pointed. The land dropped off into a steep ravine, which he could only see across, not into. He crawled back to his crutch, which was still stuck in the ground where he had fallen, then trudged toward the ravine.

The sides of the ravine were steep and he could not see down into it until he was almost at the lip. Not knowing what the gulch held, Echo had a feeling of anticipation in his belly, like he was about to see what was under the tree on Christmas morning. He inched forward, now supporting much of his exhausted body on the crutch. "Holy crap!" Echo said aloud as he reached the edge and peered in. At the bottom, some forty feet down, a tiny creek trickled.

There was nothing unusual about that. But on the other side of the ravine, on a flattened piece of ground just above the little creek, was a cluster of three boulders. Strangely, it looked as if the boulders had been placed on the flat like some ancient shrine. There were three of them—all gray and splotched with lichens and sheets of moss. They were about the size and shape of extra-large refrigerators laid on their sides.

Echo's perspective was slightly above the three boulders, so he could look down on to them from his side of the ravine. They formed a perimeter in the shape of a three-sided arrowhead—just like the arrowhead on the Lenape turtle symbol. The point was facing uphill, directly to the north. Echo blinked his eyes, not sure if his imagination was playing tricks on him. But there it was, plain as day. He could see a large open space in the center of the three boulders, almost like a rock fence, protecting some special room-like area at the center. Echo shook like one of Luna's excited coon dogs, ready to light out on a hunt. This was it! It had to be it! And he had to get over there! But, how? It was forty feet, nearly straight down to the bottom of the ravine, and he had but one useful leg. He might get down, but he'd never get out without some climbing system.

He had twenty feet of quarter-inch nylon rope in his pack. That would get him halfway. But what about the last twenty feet? He could make strong cordage from the inner bark of tulip poplar, but that would take forever. He could search for some wild grapevine to extend his rope, but he didn't remember seeing any nearby. *How can I turn twenty feet of rope into forty?* he thought. The image of a chain with links crossed his mind, and an idea began to form.

Echo found two quaking aspen saplings the diameter of cardboard toilet paper tubes. He cut a straight ten-foot section from each tree, trimmed them clean of branches, and dragged them back to the lip of the ravine. He didn't feel too bad about cutting the aspen. It was a pioneer tree of the forest and grew fast from a wide spreading root system that connected many trees together. He also chose aspen because it was soft and easy to work. With a drill bit-like tool called an awl that he kept in his kit, he bored a hole through each end of one pole about two inches from the tip. On the other pole, he did the same, but only on one end. He pulled the rope from his pack and laid his knife next to it. Echo hated cutting rope. A long piece of rope had many uses; a short piece of rope . . . not so much. He hoped his idea would work.

He uncoiled the rope and cut it into two halves. He tied one-half to a stout sugar maple that stood on the ravine's lip. He tied the other end through one of the holes in an aspen pole. He grabbed the second piece of rope and tied it through the hole on the other end of the first pole. Finally, he tied the remaining end through the hole of the second aspen pole. Now he had a forty foot long "chain" made of rope and aspen poles. He threw the chain over the edge of the ravine, the weight of the poles pulling the contraption all the way down. The last pole dangled three feet above the ravine floor. *Perfect*, he thought.

He lashed his crutch to the outside of his backpack and started down. Hand over hand, he lowered himself, using his good leg to push himself away from the ravine wall. The going was fairly easy with gravity in his favor. His foot throbbed and he tried not to think about what going back up would be like. For now, in his mind, he was a rock climber, repelling some famous escarpment.

About halfway down, something told him to look up. There! Standing beside the tree where his rope was tied, three coyotes peered down at him. Strangely, Echo was not scared. He froze and tried not to make eye contact. They looked more curious than threatening. Echo hoped he could keep it that way by not meeting their gaze. Coyotes rarely bothered humans unless they felt threatened. Then again, he was in an awfully unusual position. Perhaps the coyotes would see him as lunch on a string. The two on the outside reminded him of medium-sized dogs, perhaps forty pounds. The one in the middle, though, was a whole different story. He was a foot taller than the other two, and thick muscles rippled in his neck and chest. But that wasn't even the most striking thing. His face was drenched in fresh, shiny blood, and his left ear was nothing but a healed-over stump, like it had been bitten off in some long-ago battle with a rival. "Ole One Ear" was clearly a fighter. Suddenly, the coyote on Ole One Ear's right whined softly, a vocalization that signaled danger. Then the coyotes were gone in a blur of rich brown fur.

Before continuing, Echo hung breathlessly for a minute, his arms aching from holding his weight. In the bottom of the ravine, he unlashed his crutch and hurried—as best he could—to the three boulders. A gap between the giant rocks on the lower west side invited him to enter the protected arrowhead-shaped space. *Nothing* could have prepared him for what he found inside. Echo staggered back, leaning hard on his crutch to keep his feet under him. For a long time he did not move, his mind trying to calculate what he was seeing. A strong, clear voice—a man's voice—cut the air. "What the hell?" It took several heartbeats before Echo realized it was his own voice, his own mind reacting without thought to what was before him.

He took a few steps forward and lifted one of the many elk antlers that surrounded a large, flat stone at the center of the space. There were dozens of black crow feathers too, like they'd been plucked from so many wings. Some of the antlers and feathers were weathered, suggesting they had been there for decades, while others seemed to have been placed there recently. This was not random. Someone had been bringing sacred objects to this shrine for a very long time.

And there was more evidence of recent human presence. The center of each of the three boulders was marked with a Lenape turtle symbol, neatly done by hand with fresh red and black paint. The arrows on the turtle symbols all pointed the same direction—counterclockwise around the shrine. The center stone was the most astonishing. It was perfectly round, about the size of a large trash can lid, and sat exactly in the middle of the triangular space. On the flat stone was painted a young, defiant-looking Lenape woman riding on the back of a majestic bull elk. She had long, flowing black hair. Three black crows were perched on her thrust-out left arm. Each crow looked in a slightly different direction, so no matter where Echo stood, it seemed like he was being watched. The sensation was creepy and made his heart race. If he had the energy and two good legs, he might have run away and never looked back!

18

BOOT CAMP

Monday, September 6th

6:45 a.m.

Summer seemed to disappear before Echo's eyes. He had enjoyed the many things that kids do: playing baseball with his friends, swimming in the deep hole down at the creek, fishing at the lake, and even camping with his family. But through it all, his Sure Enough Mountain Man trip was never far from his mind. It had taken a lot of convincing, but one evening in early summer, Echo's mom had finally said "yes" and from that point on, Echo was consumed with preparing for what would be the trip of a lifetime.

He practiced with his bow until he was hitting a soda can every time at twenty yards. Sometimes he coaxed his sister into throwing homemade cardboard discs into the air. In a remarkable show of skill, Echo would knock the discs to the ground without really thinking about it . . . or even aiming. When Rachel threw, Echo seemed to know instinctively when to release the arrow so it centered the flying disc. He just raised his bow and shot in one fluid motion. It was a thing to see. Echo's skill with the bow caught the attention of his friends and family, and they even teased him about being the next Fred Bear or maybe even an Olympic archer. Echo acted embarrassed, but deep down he secretly liked the attention. And better yet, now he knew he could get food, like rabbits and squirrels, with his homemade bow.

He spent countless sweaty afternoons in the woods behind their cabin doing bushcraft. Practicing his Smarts and Ways as he thought of it. He taught himself to put up a tarp shelter and a debris hut. He practiced starting a fire with a flint rock and steel striker. This task he found to be much harder than expected, and he eventually learned to carry shredded yellow birch bark in an old Altoids candy tin. The resin-filled bark ignited with the smallest of sparks and was a lifesaver in wet conditions. He carved cooking utensils from black cherry wood, cooked fish on a flat rock over the fire, and learned to forage for wild edible plants, like stinging nettles, chicken-of-the-woods mushrooms, and cattail roots. By August, Echo figured there weren't many people in the county—maybe even the whole state—who could do what he could. This brought him great inner pride, but he stayed humble, never allowing himself to be boastful about his skills.

114

One day at the swimming hole, his friend Buster Brasher was busting his chops about spending so much time geeking out over bushcraft stuff. Buster thought it was stupid. "Why spend so much time doing things the hard way when you could just buy a tent and some plastic silverware at Wal-Mart?" Buster said that if *he* needed to start a fire, he'd get a pocket lighter and wad of newspaper . . ..and if that didn't work, he'd rub two sticks together like they do on TV. Echo laughed at this nonsense and invited Buster to test his skills in the woods behind their cabin. After an hour with a lighter and two bundles of old newspapers, Buster still didn't have a fire that would stay going once the paper died out. Red-faced and stinking like a dumpster fie, Buster abruptly pulled his cell phone from his pocket, claiming his mom had texted him for dinner. He stormed off in a huff, and Echo didn't hear from him for several days. *That'll teach him*, thought Echo.

The Labor Day holiday usually fell in early September and marked the end of summer fun. This year, Echo's dad declared Labor Day to be Mountain Man Boot Camp Day. The idea was for his dad and Uncle Leo to put Echo's skills to the test, have a look at his gear, and go over the route for Echo's Sure Enough Mountain Man trip.

Dad and Uncle Leo had been his teachers since he'd been born. He looked up to them and didn't want to disappoint them. While Uncle Leo and his dad were brothers and had a lot in common, they were also quite different. Echo's dad was a professional wildlife scientist, naturalist, and expert hunter, especially with a recurve bow. He approached everything with a scientific lens and was very systematic about life. His Uncle Leo was more of a free agent.

Leo was four years younger than Echo's dad and had skipped the whole university thing for what he called "Back-country College." After high school, Uncle Leo spent four years trekking all over the country, backpacking, hunting, and fishing. He lived out of the back of an old Toyota pickup truck and "ate off the land." He learned to make do with whatever lay beyond his tailgate. Echo's dad said, "Uncle Leo could live on roasted grasshoppers and sleep in a hollow log for a year before he realized he was cold and hungry. Echo's mom was more straightforward when it came to Leo. She always said, "Your Uncle Leo is nuttier than a squirrel turd!" Echo always laughed no matter how many times she said it.

Echo knew that Mountain Man Boot Camp wasn't just for fun. His mom and dad had warned him that if they felt he wasn't ready, they would cancel his trip. His mom said it just wouldn't be safe if he didn't have the right skills and mindset. Echo had told everyone at school about his big trip and how he'd return a different person. How embarrassing would it be if his parents didn't even let him go? His trip was in mid-October, just few weeks away. Was he really ready?

When the day of boot camp came, Echo's dad and Uncle Leo had three stations set up in the woods behind the cabin. Each station had a different challenge that Echo would have to complete: shelter building, water acquisition, and fire starting. They ate a quick breakfast and started just after sunup. It was a perfect morning, with fall's nip in the air and the Virginia creeper coming into full glory, like someone spiraled red holiday garland around all the oak trees in their woods.

At station one, Echo's dad described the challenge in his best boot camp, drill sergeant voice. He said, "In wilderness survival, you need a good shelter to keep you warm and dry.

Under many circumstances, you can't live more than a few days without a roof over your head. In this scenario, you've been on a day hike in early spring. It's forty-five degrees, starting to rain, and you're lost. You must stay the night in the woods. In your pack is a small emergency tarp and some parachute cord. Your challenge is to erect a rainproof shelter as fast as possible."

No problemo, thought Echo. His favorite tarp shelter was something called a "plow point," and he'd practiced it many times.

Uncle Leo called out, "On your mark, get set, go!"

Echo quickly but calmly evaluated the site and made a plan. He found an oak branch on the forest floor and cut it into three eight-inch pieces with a folding saw, then sharpened them into tent stakes with his hatchet. Next, using a bowline knot, he tied one corner of the tarp to a tree with parachute cord. Then he secured the other three tarp corners to the ground with his homemade tent stakes so the tarp was pulled tight. He took one big step away from the shelter's opening, scraped a spot with the heel of his boot, and yelled, "Done!"

Uncle Leo looked impressed and said, "Twelve minutes, thirty-six seconds. Not bad at all, but what was that little step thing you did at the end?"

"That's the right distance for a fire to be safe but still keep you warm through the night," Echo replied.

Uncle Leo looked at his brother and said, "Woohoo, this kid is good!"

Now they moved to station two, and Ted Orion began barking orders like a drill sergeant again. "A human can survive only three days without water. You cannot live without water, son. It's a biological fact. And in case you were wondering . . . drinking your own pee won't work either. Pee is full of toxins from your body. The yellow stuff won't change your luck, so close your zipper and figure out something else."

Echo burst out laughing, and his dad shot him a fake serious look and continued. "In this scenario, you've been stranded with no water after a plane crash on a dry mountaintop. You have a plastic water bottle you salvaged from the plane, which is empty of course."

Yuck, Echo thought. Plastic stuff was terrible for the environment and he hated it. But it was everywhere . . . even in many survival situations.

"GO!" shouted Uncle Leo.

After just a few minutes, Echo's hands were flying. With his belt knife, he cut the top one-third from the water bottle, leaving him with what looked like a plastic cup and a funnel. He poked one hole on each side near the top of the cup. He moved to a large piece of wild grapevine that hung in a loop near the ground but was connected up in the treetops. Echo cut a V-shaped notch at the lowest point in the loop. Gravity-fed water immediately began dripping to the ground. Next, he took one of his boot laces and tied it through the holes in the plastic cup to make something like a tiny bucket with a handle. He tied the bucket under the dripping water to capture it. Drip, drip. The cup began to fill.

Now he stuffed the cutoff funnel end of the water bottle with sphagnum moss that he gathered from some large, shaded rocks. With his fingers, he pushed on the moss like it was a wet sponge until water oozed out the small end of the funnel. This added about two ounces to the cup hanging from the grapevine. "Done!" cried Echo. In eight minutes flat, Echo had collected six ounces of water. At that pace, he could easily collect the thirty-two ounces a person needed to survive every day.

On to station three. The fire test. Gulp! Echo saw nothing but a piece of flint and a steel striker laid out on a stump. No tinder. No kindling. And certainly no artificial material like cotton balls laced with Vaseline, which lit as easily as a candle. Before Echo could fret any more, drill sergeant Dad started in. "A person can die of exposure in three hours. Hypothermia is a horrible way to go. And you need fire to sterilize water and cook food. In short, pilgrim, even the toughest Mountain Man won't make it long in the wilderness without fire. Here's the scenario. You are stranded on an Alaska mountainside. A storm has set in, with wind howling out of the northwest."

With that, Uncle Leo walked to a suspicious looking brush pile, reached in, and fiddled with something. Suddenly, wind gusted across the top of the ground and leaves shot into the air. A fan! *Those doggone tricksters!* Echo thought to himself.

Uncle Leo gave a wry grin and pointed to a spot straight downwind of the fan. "Here's where your fire goes," he said. "Now you have twenty minutes to go from zero to hero. The clock is ticking."

If Echo knew anything, it was that panic was unproductive. Being successful took a calm approach. The first thing he needed was a wind break from that blasted fan of Uncle Leo's. With rocks and short pieces of logs, he made a *U* shape on the ground with the closed end of the *U* blocking the wind of the fan.

Now he needed fuel. He knew that he could make hot sparks from the flint and steel. What he lacked was fine, dry material to serve as tinder. He needed a tinder bundle to take his spark. He quickly searched the forest high and low, grabbing small, dry sticks for kindling as he trotted along. Finally, he spotted a place where a tree had fallen the previous summer. Protected underneath were dry grasses and the feathery heads of goldenrod plants. He gathered a few handfuls and headed back to his fire spot.

He divided his kindling into small, medium, and large pieces. Next, he laid three of the medium-sized sticks inside the windbreak to lift the fire above the wet ground. He wondered how much time had passed. He had only twenty minutes and had probably used more than half gathering material. If he couldn't make fire on his first try, then he'd certainly run out of time. There was no way his parents would let him go on the trip if he failed at making fire.

Echo fluffed the dry gasses and crushed goldenrod heads into what looked like a loose bird's nest with a hollow at the middle for catching sparks. He placed the nest on the kindling and crouched over it to block even more of the wind. His first several attempts produced only weak sparks that died before reaching the nest. Panic turned to carelessness, and with a wild strike, his hand hit the nest, tossing it into the wind, where it scattered. In desperation, Echo glanced at his dad, who calmly said, "You can do it, Echo. Keep trying." Echo rebuilt the nest and took a deep breath. He guessed that only seconds remained before Uncle Leo would yell, "Time's up."

He struck twice with the same pitiful sparks dying in the air. He remembered something Luna had told him. "Always use the sharpest edge of your flint." Echo turned the flint in his hand, choosing a new side with a thin, sharp edge. This time, hot sparks showered into the nest, producing an ember. He scooped the nest to his face, gently blowing on the fragile orange glow. Smoke billowed, and the nest puffed into flame! He placed the little fireball back on the kindling and began adding small sticks.

"TIME!" yelled Uncle Leo. Echo shot into the air and pumped his fist. He'd done it. He'd made fire in a windstorm on an Alaska mountain! Even Uncle Leo was jumping up and down like a little kid.

Back at their cabin, Echo excitedly told his mom and Rachel how he'd beaten every challenge, even Uncle Leo's wind machine! After lunch, they sat at the dining room table with a laptop computer and a stack of old-school topographic maps. The idea was to map out the route for Echo's trip. Olivia Orion knew the trails and landmarks around the Pennsylvania Wilds as well as anyone. She traced lines with her finger and pointed to important spots. Echo secretly tried to steer the route toward the valley that held Young Woman's Creek, where he thought the second Book of Lenape Way was hidden. But his mom insisted on a safer trail that was nearly two miles away through unbroken timber. Before long, it was settled. This trip was a lot for his mom to accept, and Echo knew that if he argued, she might pull the plug altogether. He had to accept her trail. The plan was now in place.

19

ELK HIDE BUNDLE

Friday, October 15th

3:02 p.m.

The boulder shrine was just plain spooky with its elk antlers, crow feathers, and that crazy painting of the Lenape woman. But the part that weirded Echo out the most was knowing that someone else had been there. The turtle symbols in the shrine were different than the others he'd found. It was the same symbol alright, but these were crisp and had been recently freshened with modern paint. Who else could know about the clue Luna had given him? Did they know about the hidden Lenape book too? Were they watching him right now, this very minute, waiting to see if he would discover it? Echo realized he was clenching his teeth and took a moment to calm himself before moving deeper into the shrine's triangular space.

Trailing the fingers of his right hand against the cold wetness of the boulders, he made a full circle inside the shrine. As he walked, he kept the painting on the center rock in his vision. The crows on the Lenape woman's arm still seemed to be eyeing him from every angle. It was like they'd been put there to guard the place. Then he stopped abruptly. Something wasn't right. It was just a feeling at first, but then something moved . . ..a shadow perhaps. He tensed, and his breath grew ragged. Someone was coming. He looked for a place to hide, but there was nothing. He was cornered. Trapped with no escape route. Suddenly, *CAW-CAW.* A crow's piercing call splintered the cold air just over Echo's head. The menacing black bird was perched on a tree branch overhanging the shrine, its shadow going up and down like footsteps with the bobbing of the branch. The crow peered down, directly into Echo. Not past him and not at him, but into him. Into his very soul. Then it flapped off—gone as quickly as it had appeared. "What have I done?" Echo muttered to himself. Whatever it was, it was too late. He couldn't turn back now.

The answer had to be hidden in that center rock. In that EXACT SPOT was the very point on all of Earth where the *spirit of the crow and the elk flowed together with the young woman.* It was plainly painted for all to see. This had to be it. Echo dropped to his knees and began feeling around the rock for a hidden compartment . . . for anything that might be large enough to hold the second Lenape Book of Ways. But nothing. It was solid rock. No hidden buttons or false doors like in the movies.

"It must be buried underneath the rock," Echo mumbled to himself. He was overcome with the thought of finding the book. He didn't care about the scary crow or anything else. His job—his duty to Luna—was to find the dang book. Using the tip of his crutch, he dug wildly at the soil around the edge of the rock, flinging clods of dirt high into the air. Suddenly, without warning, an earsplitting *CAW-CAW* rang out. Echo looked up. The crow looked down, straight into Echo again. A feeling like a caterpillar walking on his bare skin rose up Echo's spine. *This is a lousy idea*, he thought. *I'm in someone's shrine, Someone's sacred place, digging someone's sacred dirt. This is wrong. I shouldn't be here.*

The crow seemed to sense Echo's change of heart. It fluffed its feathers and began preening. Calmly, it smoothed each of its wing feathers with the tip of its black bill. It seemed to be saying, "Go on, keep digging; I'm watching." After several swipes with the crutch near the front of the rock, the soil gave way and the crutch plunged into some sort of opening. This was it! There *was* a secret space hidden beneath the rock! Using the crutch like a pry bar, Echo lifted up on the free end with all his strength, but the rock didn't budge. He repositioned himself, now with his shoulder under the crutch for more leverage. He tried again, and just like that, the rock slid forward, exposing the hidden compartment.

CAW-CAW-CAW. The crow became excited, giving raucous calls and rattling sounds. The hidden compartment beneath the rock was perfectly square—a hole dug into the earth, twelve inches on each side and lined with flat stones on the sides and bottom—like a square well without the water. The compartment held a large bundle made from layers of elk hide, waterproofed with bear tallow, and tied tightly with leg sinew from a deer. Echo gently lifted the bundle from the compartment and set it aside on the ground. A smaller compartment was hidden beneath the bundle. In it was a box, beautifully made from freshwater mussel shells. It was like a small jewelry box with a perfectly fitted lid.

Echo sat the box next to the elk hide bundle and slid the center rock back over the hidden compartment. He packed dirt around the rock as neatly as he could. He wanted to leave this sacred place the way he found it. He stared at the bundle and the box. The mussel shells had been polished and shone purple-blue in the light. What was inside? He needed to know . . .*had* to know. But these were not his things. The bundle. The box. They were not his, did not even belong to his people. These were Lenape things. For Lenape people. He suddenly felt guilty for even being there. He'd followed the clues to solve a mystery. But why him?

CAW-CAW. The crow was in flight now, and it too seemed agitated with his presence. It swooped aggressively at Echo, blowing his hair back with razor-close passes, then it repeatedly flew in the direction of Echo's shelter. He got the hint. It was time to go. He placed the bundle in his backpack and the fragile box in his jacket pocket. "Goodbye, crow," he shouted as he squeezed between the boulders and back out into the forest.

On his way out of the boulder shrine, Echo noticed an electronic trail camera mounted on a tree. It was like the ones that Buster Brasher's family used to monitor deer trails. The cameras were tripped by heat and movement, and since Echo had just walked in front of it, he knew that someone now had his picture. Was that someone just a deer hunter or the "keeper of the shrine?" There was nothing to do about it now, he had to move on.

It was nearly dark when Echo reached his shelter. He looked around for boot prints or other signs that someone might have been looking for him, but saw nothing. He had banked the fire before leaving. Red-hot coals remained beneath the covering of ash, and with only modest coaxing, Echo had a crackling fire. The excitement of his experience at the boulder shrine had distracted him from the worst of his hunger pangs, but now they were back to punish him. It was dark, and he was too exhausted to hunt anyway. He thought of something his Uncle Leo often said: "What doesn't kill you makes you stronger." If that were true, and his stomach didn't eat him alive, he would be the man of steel by sunup.

Echo wanted another look at the elk hide bundle and mussel-shell box before going to bed.

The bundle smelled strongly of mildew mixed with the sweet fragrance of old leather, like a baseball glove that drew damp from being left outside too long. The outer layer of hide had begun to rot, causing soft pieces of the brown skin to flake off in his lap. Something about the bundle—its shape, its weight—reminded Echo of the Bible his grandmother kept on a little bookshelf. The sinew ran around the bundle one way and then the other, so all four sides were held tightly. It would have to be cut open, and then there would be no putting it back together. He pictured Luna sawing at the tough sinew with one of her chert knives.

The mussel-shell box was in every way the opposite of the bundle. It was rigid, fragile, and held no odor. Firelight danced off the purplish shells, rivaling the beauty of any pearl. Echo remembered reading how Native American tribes made beautiful beads, called wampum, from mussel shells. They used wampum as a form of money to trade for animal pelts, stone tools, and food. This worked until Whites arrived and began mass producing wampum, which made the Indian's wampum worthless and had the side effect of driving many mussel species to near extinction. Even today, scientists were trying to rebuild mussel populations that were wiped out in the 1800s.

Echo slid the box back into his jacket pocket and was returning the bundle to his backpack when he noticed something white near the opening of his pack. A small envelope was stuck to the zipper. It must have been pulled up from the bottom of his pack when he withdrew the bundle. The outside said "Echo" in his mom's handwriting. She probably sneaked it into his pack where it had gotten lost on the bottom for the past six days.

Inside was a goofy family photo they took near a waterfall on a summer camping trip. A handwritten note read, "Dear Echo, have fun, good luck, and most of all, be careful. I will miss you. Love, Mom." At the bottom she wrote "And into the forest you go, to lose your mind and find your soul." Echo couldn't remember for sure, but he thought this was something the famous naturalist John Muir had once said. His mom always loved the saying. Whether he was a boy or a man didn't matter right now. Echo wept quiet tears for his mom and all of his family. He was alive and getting better, but they didn't know that. Maybe they thought he was already dead. He wanted to be able to tell them, *I'm right here. I'm okay. I did something really amazing.* Most of all, he missed them more than he thought he could miss anything.

He wiped his eyes, stoked the fire, and crawled into his sleeping bag . . . the photo and note held tight to his chest.

20

NECK KNIFE

Friday, October 8th

6:30 p.m.

Echo's final week of school before leaving for his Sure Enough Mountain Man trip felt like watching paint dry. Every torturous day went slower than the last, but he needed to focus. His parents were required to get special permission to take him out of school for a week. Not wanting to disappoint anyone or jeopardize his trip, Echo worked extra hard so that he could come back to school in good standing. When Friday finally rolled around, he was ready to bust loose. He sprinted down the hall with his outstretched fingers rippling along every locker as he went.

His parents had organized a "good-luck party" on Friday night before he would officially hit the woods on Saturday morning. Echo had asked his dad to invite Luna, but she wouldn't come. She said she wouldn't be comfortable around a lot of people. She said her place was in the woods with the trees and four-legged animals…not the two-legged ones. Echo was disappointed, but he understood. Luna had her ways, and that was that. Truth be known, Echo preferred the woods to most people too.

After school, Echo carefully went through all of his gear for the trip. When it came to wilderness survival, his Dad always said, "Two is one and one is none." Echo took his advice and carried backups of important items in case one got lost or broken. Echo went down his checklist: hatchet, belt knife, folding saw, multi-tool, flint and steel, flashlight, cooking pot, water bottle, tarp, parachute cord, bedroll, sleeping bag, fishing line, fishhooks, extra clothes, maps, salt and pepper, packs of oatmeal, small bag of rice, venison jerky, two-way radio, and extra batteries.

Satisfied it was all there, he loaded it in the back of his dad's pickup truck. Last, but certainly not least, Echo laid his hickory bow and a dozen dogwood arrows on the truck seat. The bow had become his most prized possession and the thing he would count on most for survival. His arrows were tipped with razor sharp, chert arrowheads that Luna had taught him how to make. Six were large enough to kill big game, and the rest suited for smaller animals, like chipmunks.

Around six p.m., the guests began arriving at the Orions' cabin. Everyone was carrying some sort of food to share. There were Echo's grandparents, Uncle Leo, Buster and his family, Billy Tyson, and several other friends from school. For the occasion, Ted Orion had hauled an entire white-tailed deer hindquarter from the freezer. He slow-roasted it in a homemade cooker fired with chunks of oak and hickory wood. They ate the venison alongside mounds of sweet and salty homemade baked beans, creamy potato salad, and roasted apples. They even had slices of chewy bread, baked from cattail flour that Luna had sent over.

Everyone was eager to talk with Echo about his trip. He politely made the rounds, answering their questions. A few people said he was crazy, his grandparents were worried about him, but most everyone showed admiration and wished him well. Buster's mom, who always dressed fancy and wore a lot of makeup, wanted to know what Echo knew about that looney Luna Woapalanne. In a sneering tone, she said, "So, Echo, I hear you've been hanging out with that crazy old woman who lives in the woods. I don't know why she brags about being related to Indians. Those people weren't exactly innocent, you know. I don't think having Indian blood is something to be proud of."

Echo felt his own blood boil and thought he might strangle this woman right here in his own backyard. Fortunately, his dad was nearby and overhead the conversation. Ted Orion piped in with a firm tone directed at Buster's mom, "Luna is a fine woman, and the Native Americans were only defending their way of life and retaliating against all of our broken treaties."

Buster's mom looked repulsed before lifting her nose in the air and turning on one heel as she sauntered off to find Buster. *Good riddance*, thought Echo.

Ted put a strong arm around his son and smiled at him. "I'm proud of you, Echo. You're doing the right thing. Don't let people like her get you down." Echo appreciated his dad's support, but he was still baffled . . . and more than a little ticked off by how some people believed it was okay to destroy others just because they were different. What was so hard about being kind and keeping your word?

Echo thought about the story that Luna told him about the Mountain Man and Native American woman who were faced with crossing the same flooded river. While they chose different strategies and neither was successful in hunting buffalo, they respected each other's choices. But Echo knew the history between Native Americans and Whites had never been a simple one.

His relationship with Luna had enticed Echo into watching a lot of YouTube videos and reading books about Native American history. He learned that from 1778 to 1881, 368 peace treaties had been signed between Indian tribes and the US Government. Most of the treaties involved some deal where the government would give the Indian tribes trade goods, like cooking pots and blankets, in exchange for their land. Or the government would agree to leave the Indians alone if they could just have a little more land for their settlements. Many of the treaties were false promises from the day they were signed, and all were eventually broken, leading to constant warfare between Indians and Whites.

Echo also knew that the first of these bad treaties was signed with Luna's very own tribe, the Lenape. It was called the Treaty of Fort Pitt and was signed in 1778, just one year before Chief Bald Eagle was killed. The treaty promoted peace and trust between the Lenape and the new White settlers, but it never worked. Tensions grew as the Whites pushed ever deeper into Lenape territory and stole their food. The relationship shattered when a group of Pennsylvania militiamen massacred ninety-six Lenape women and children at a village in Ohio.

Probably the most horrible thing Echo learned was that the US government intentionally killed millions of American bison (buffalo) on the Great Plains to "starve out" the

Indians. It was like they were exterminating rats. For thousands of years, hunting buffalo had been a way of life for Plains Indians. They used the buffalo for food, clothing, blankets, teepees; they even used the bones for tools. Everything depended on the buffalo. Without them, the Indians withered up and died like flowers without water. Greed and narrowmindedness, Echo decided, were the roots of all evil.

Echo was becoming more anxious for morning and the start of his trip. He wanted a good night's sleep, so he wasn't exactly happy when he saw a new guest arriving late to the party. It was just getting dark when headlights flickered off the trees along the driveway. As the vehicle drew closer, something about it looked familiar. Then Echo could hear the bay of coon dogs. It was Luna's truck! Luna was here! He raced to the driveway to meet her.

The old woman didn't get out, but talked to Echo through the open truck window. "How's your party, child?" Luna asked.

"It's okay," replied Echo. "I kinda just want to get on with my trip."

There was an uncomfortable pause before Luna spoke. "I can't stay . . . On my way up to Chestnut Flats to see if Boone and Crockett can get the better of Old Jed." Old Jed was a big, crafty raccoon that Luna had been chasing for over a year but could never catch. He always managed to slip the dogs. Echo couldn't decide if Luna was really after Old Jed or whether she just liked to wander on Chestnut Flats at night, remembering all the times she spent there with her father.

"Echo, listen to me," said the old woman. "I don't want you looking for that book without me. It's too dangerous. I know your trip will take you close to Young Woman's Creek, but it's not safe on your own." Luna and Echo had only known each other for less than a year, but it was like she always knew exactly what he was thinking.

He smiled and nodded. "I won't," he said.

"Good. Gotta go. Old Jed's waitin'," Luna said with a wry grin. She put the truck in reverse and started to back away, but then suddenly slammed on the brakes. Through the windshield, Echo saw her arm move up and to the left as she slid the ancient truck's shifter back into park.

The interior light came on as Luna stepped out. From her silhouette, you'd never guess Luna's age. She was straight as a locust fence post and tougher than barbed wire. She awkwardly approached Echo. "I dang near forgot, child," she said. She withdrew something from the pocket of her overalls and handed it to Echo. It was dark, but Echo could feel it well enough to know what it was. A neck knife.

"Is this what you've been working on in secret?" he asked.

"Yes," Luna replied. "Wear it always as a symbol of strength. It will save your tail when it most needs saving."

The two stood, facing one another without being able to see each other's faces in the night. Abruptly, Luna bent to Echo's height and wrapped her arms around him. It was a quick hug, and Echo didn't have time to hug back. "Good luck and keep to the plan, child," Luna hollered as she jacked her tall body back into the truck.

"Thank you!" Echo yelled over the raucous barking of the dogs.

On the walk back to the house, Echo felt something wet on his cheek. He smiled. The old woman might be tough as barbed wire, but her heart was as warm as a campfire.

21

OLE ONE EAR AND THE BUCK

Saturday, October 16th

6:21 a.m.

Echo awoke with a start and glanced around his shelter. His heart raced, but why? Was it a bad dream? After his brush with the crow in the boulder shrine the day before, a nightmare or two could certainly be expected. His shelter was very dark. No light shone around the edges of the door or through his tarp roof. The internal rhythm of his body told Echo that it was morning, but not morning enough for daylight. What had woken him, he wondered. Echo sat up with his sleeping bag still around him and poked mindlessly at the ashes of his spent fire. There wasn't much he could do in the dark, so he lay back down to think.

He realized he was not afraid. He was enveloped in black darkness with no modern conveniences, no light switch to snap on. This fact alone would bring many people to their knees. But there was much more. Echo was also stranded in the forest and no one knew where he was. He should be terrified of what might happen. Most people would be wetting their pants! Yet, Echo was not afraid. Anxious, yes. He desperately wanted to see his family. But he was not afraid.

Echo's mom was a strong woman. She taught him a lot about what was worth fearing and what was not. Olivia Orion said there were irrational fears, like being afraid of a harmless eastern garter snake just because it was a snake. Some people were even afraid of pictures of snakes. Now that was irrational! "But the fear you most need to think about," said Olivia, "is rational fear."

Rational fear was being afraid of the things that really could hurt you . . . or even kill you! Being hit by a bus could crush you. White water canoeing could drown you. Getting in between a mother moose and her calf could get you trampled. These were things to be afraid of—or perhaps more accurately, these were things to think about. It all came down to fear of the unknown, Echo's mom liked to say. If you understand something, if you really know it, you can't be afraid of it. "Knowing is strength," Olivia would say. Echo figured this is why he wasn't afraid. He knew the woods inside and out. He understood the risks and how to manage them. There was no fear, only respect.

Echo sat up in his sleeping bag again. What was that? He heard a sound in the distance. Perhaps it was the same sound that had woken him in the first place. He held his breath to quiet the noise of his breathing. There it was again. A soft yipping coming from the direction of Young Woman's Creek. A few seconds later, a much louder yip replied from somewhere near his shelter. Then, a third yip sounded off from farther up the creek. Echo scrambled to his feet. He understood what was happening and what would be coming next. Soon, all hell would break loose!

It was a pack of coyotes "talking" to each other. They were getting organized to make an attack on some prey animal. Their yipping was like the blowing of a bugle just before an army charged its enemy. Then, there it was! The darkness cracked open with bloodcurdling yowls, yips, and snarls. The yipping became more frantic and louder as the pack closed in. Echo could picture the coyotes tightening the circle on some doomed animal as it danced in circles looking for an escape route. Then came the sound of running and crashing as the pack chased its prey directly by Echo's shelter. He imagined the curled lips and white, popping teeth of the coyotes as they zigzagged madly to corral their prey for the kill. Echo wondered if Ole One Ear, the big coyote he'd seen near the boulder shrine, was among the pack.

He pictured the wide-eyed desperation on the face of whatever animal was running just beyond the reach of the coyotes' deadly jaws. The vicious sounds grew louder before fading into the distance as the bloodthirsty pack moved passed Echo's shelter and off to the east. Then, a single, feeble *blaaaat* reached Echo's ears before all fell quiet. The sound was weak and shaky—a final gasp of defeat that most likely meant death. With this last sound, Echo knew that it was a deer the coyotes had brought down. In his mind's eye, he saw the deer struggling to stay on its feet, being pulled to its belly by a half dozen hungry sets of teeth, going blank in the face, submitting to its fate, and finally lowering its wet, brown eyes to the ground. He wondered, *Was it a buck, was it a doe, or even more likely, a yearling deer that had been born just that spring?*

It really didn't matter. There was no time to be sad. Whatever it was, it meant food for the coyotes and for Echo too . . . if he could only get there and chase the coyotes off before they devoured their meal.

The sun was coming up now and he had to work fast. Without thinking, Echo pulled a boot onto his injured right foot and found that it fit! It was still very tender and he couldn't walk without his crutch, but at least he could wear a boot. That was progress.

He slipped out of the shelter door with his bow and the six dogwood arrows tipped with razor-sharp stone points suited for big game. His only plan was to follow the trail made by the churning pack of predators. He'd figure out the rest when he got there.

He had no trouble reading the deep pockmarks made by the frantic deer and the wild scuffs created from zigzagging coyotes. After 100 yards, Echo came upon a place where the deer had stumbled and the coyotes had momentarily driven their teeth into its flesh. The spot was clear of leaves where an intense battle had raged. Droplets of bright red arterial blood spattered the bare soil, like a child had dropped a cherry snow cone.

Echo knelt and dipped his fingers in the sticky blood. Impulsively, he sniffed it. The metallic odor triggered a primitive impulse somewhere deep inside of him. The excitement of the chase, combined with his intense need to eat, had flipped a psychological switch. Suddenly, he understood in a new way why his dad and Uncle Leo hunted. Why Luna chased raccoons. The need to eat. The need to hunt. The need to stay connected to the rhythm of the natural world was undeniable. It was in all of us.

Echo felt his posture change. No longer was he walking upright. He nocked an arrow on his bow's string and crouch-walked, keeping an eye on the ground for blood and scanning ahead for the pack. He didn't look for the whole pack or even an entire coyote. He looked for the swish of a bushy tail or the triangular shape of an ear. By the time he saw the whole pack, it would be too late. Echo wanted to stay hidden from the coyotes for as long as he could. He knew they would not accept him, but he yearned to move among them, to be part of the pack.

Yip-yip-yowwwl! A triumphant coyote call suddenly vibrated the air . . . and it was close, just over the knoll that lay ahead! Echo's crouch became deeper as he moved among the trees for cover. Near the crest of the knoll, he began belly-crawling, pushing his bow ahead and dragging his bad leg behind. He was not prepared for the grizzly scene before him when he peeked over the rise.

Twenty yards ahead, six coyotes had their heads buried in the rapidly disappearing body of a small white-tailed deer buck. Echo could hear lapping, sucking, and tearing sounds as the pack pulled greenish-silvery entrails from the stomach cavity. He smelled the sweet-foul scent of the buck's fermented stomach contents and even the wet-dog aroma of the coyotes themselves.

Suddenly a flash of movement caught his eye. Ten yards to the left of the feasting pack, another coyote excitedly paced and made short lunges at something in a stand of mountain laurel. It was Ole One Ear, a full three feet tall, muscles rippling under his gray-brown coat. There was no doubt he was the leader, the alpha male of the pack. Then, Echo saw another coyote with Ole One Ear. This one was big too, and Echo figured it for Ole One Ear's mate, the alpha female. It took him a half minute to see what was happening amid the tangled laurel branches.

A mature, eight-point buck was fighting for his life. His right front leg was broken and blood streamed from his neck and sides. Its tongue lolled from the side of its mouth. The buck was exhausted, but fought back with great thrusts of his pointed antlers.

The two alphas were keeping this bucked pinned down while the rest of the family filled their bellies.

They were experienced with the dangers of a mature buck. An antler tine to the chest would mean sure death for a coyote. Ole One Ear and his mate worked as a team, timing their lunges to keep the buck off-balance and deftly staying away from the crown of antlers. Soon, the whole pack would descend on the eight-point for the kill. Echo had to act fast.

He backed away, circling the knoll so he could come at the injured buck from the back side, with the wind and cover in his favor. Crawling forward, fifty yards, forty yards, thirty yards, and then twenty yards. Finally, only ten yards separated Echo from the buck! Ole One Ear and his mate were distracted and never saw him coming. This was it! Echo stood with an arrow on the string and his bow at half draw. Whatever went down next would define his Sure Enough Mountain Man trip. Would he starve? Would he be rich with venison? Or would he become just another meal for Ole One Ear?

At the sight of Echo, the subordinate coyotes feeding on the smaller buck retreated into the forest. Why wouldn't they? They had full bellies and didn't need to tangle with Echo. Ole One Ear and his girl didn't see it that way.

They leapt between Echo and the injured buck. The alphas took on an aggressive posture with their necks outstretched and noses tipped up. White, curved canine teeth gleamed as the two worked a crisscross pattern to keep Echo off guard. When they were just fifteen feet away, within easy range to pounce on Echo and tear him to shreds, the crisscrossing stopped. Ole One Ear crept forward and crouched low, coiling his legs to spring for Echo's throat.

Echo did not run. Instead, he drew his bow and took aim, ready to release an arrow into the alpha's soft underbelly when he lunged from mere feet away.

Caw-caw, a crow hollered overhead, and at the same instant, a puff of wind hit Echo on the back, carrying his human scent straight to Ole One Ear. The old male instantly registered recognition of a predator greater than himself. Under pumping legs, the two alphas forfeited the buck and sped off to join the rest of the pack. Now it was just Echo and the buck, whose knees were beginning to buckle from his injuries.

Echo was already at full draw, and he knew what had to be done. He picked an imaginary spot on the buck's heaving chest, just behind his shoulder. The selfbow's string let out a hushed *whoosh* when Echo let it slip from his fingers. The dogwood arrow and its stone tip took the buck cleanly. In just five seconds, Echo watched the light go from the buck's eyes, and the stillness of death came over his body. Killing was never ever easy, and this time was no different. Echo realized how badly he was shaking; he needed to rest.

He went to the fallen buck and lay beside it, one hand on the deer's warm hide, the other still clutching his bow. Echo closed his eyes for a long time, saying nothing, thinking nothing, just letting the feelings wash over him. Then he looked directly into the glazed over eyes of the buck and said, "Thank You," in a strong and steady voice.

22

SURPRISE VISITOR

Saturday, October 16th

1:39 p.m.

Echo had been helping his dad field dress deer ever since he was old enough to walk, but this time he had to do it on his own. He knew there were two methods. The first and most commonly used was to make an incision on the deer's belly that began between the rear legs and stopped at the chest, where the ribs made a bony plate. The incision opened the abdominal cavity, giving access to the intestines, stomach, and organs, like the liver, lungs, and heart. Echo knew the only tricky part was to make sure you didn't nick the stomach, causing the gut material to leak out, which made things messy and could taint the meat.

He had no doubt that he could "gut the buck," as most people called it, but there was one big problem. This method of field dressing called for dragging the whole deer out of the woods. This was hard work, even for a full-grown person with two good legs. There was no way Echo could drag this eight-point buck that weighed perhaps twice as much as he did!

The other method of field dressing required more skill and involved breaking the deer down into manageable pieces that could be carried. This is how hunters did it with elk that were simply too big to be dragged. The technique involved skinning the hide from the animal while it lay on the ground and then taking it apart at the hip and shoulders. From years of building his natural history collection, Echo was familiar with the anatomy of four-legged animals. Amazingly, the shoulders were not connected to the rest of the body by bones. They were strapped fast by only ligaments, which could easily be cut to remove the whole appendage.

Removing the back legs took more skill, but still, if you understood how the animal was built, it wasn't difficult. In fact, it was a little like popping apart Lego blocks. Each back leg was connected to the hip with a ball and socket joint—a ball on the end of the leg bone fit into a hole on the hip. To remove the whole leg, you just had to pop the ball from the socket with the tip of your knife.

In an hour, Echo had the hide neatly peeled from the buck and laid out on the ground with the hair side down. On the flesh side of the hide, he piled the two hind quarters, two shoulders, and the other cuts of meat. The hide acted like a tarp to keep the meat clean until it could be moved.

In two more hours of steady work, Echo had transported all of the meat, the hide, and the antlers of the buck to his shelter. On his last trip to carry meat, Echo stared at the bloodstained spot where the buck had fallen. Now that the work was finished, he had some time to think about what he had done.

This was the first deer Echo had ever killed. With this act, he'd taken the life of a living creature larger than he was. A creature sophisticated enough to have not just basic instincts, but thoughts, too. Echo had seen deer chasing each other in playful ways. Could they experience joy? He'd seen does grooming their fawns. Could they feel love, or was it just the bond that helped deer families to survive?

He always thought his dad would be with him at this moment. He thought his dad would be there to help him through this crazy roller-coaster ride of ups and downs. Ending a life was never to be taken lightly. Killing dang sure didn't make you a man, but it did make you dig deep to understand yourself.

You couldn't just walk away like you did at the end of a baseball game. Heck no, this was way bigger than that. With the tip of his crutch, Echo dug a shallow grave in the exact spot where the buck had fallen. He placed the arrow that killed the buck into the hole and covered it with dirt. He held his hand to his heart for three breaths and then turned for his shelter.

Echo kindled a substantial fire outside the entrance to his shelter and then set to work. He hung the buck's hide from a low tree branch so that it would begin to dry and not spoil. He mounted the antlers to the door of his shelter. Finally, Echo hoisted all of the meat, except for one shoulder, into a tree so that predators could not easily reach it.

Echo poured some water from the creek into his cooking pot and put it on the fire to boil. From the deer shoulder, he sliced a large steak, which he cut into cubes. He dropped the cubes, along with some oyster mushrooms he found, into the boiling water for a stew. While the stew cooked, Echo arranged a spit over the fire and began roasting the entire deer shoulder. His belly had not been full in a week, and now he planned to change that. He would have a feast.

Echo stood back and looked at it all—the hide, the antlers, the meat hung high in the air, his bow leaning against a tree, a crackling fire, a deer leg on a spit, and his snug shelter. A broad smile covered his dirty face. This was a scene to make any Mountain Man or Lenape warrior proud. He had done it! He had taken everything that the wilderness threw at him and survived. No, he had thrived. He was living with nature, providing for himself. He could live out here forever. He *wanted* to live out here forever!

He was sitting by the fire and had just drained the last drops of stew into his mouth when he caught a flash of movement on his left side. Ole One Ear and his gang must be back! There was no way Echo would let them spoil his feast. Echo grabbed his bow and slipped behind his shelter. He'd wait for the brazen coyotes to approach his stash of meat and then teach them a lesson. He was crouched, waiting in dead silence, when he heard a stick pop on the other side of his shelter. Ole One Ear was approaching from his blind side.

Echo already had an arrow on the bow string and now he applied some tension. It was time to spring his trap. He counted off in his head, one, two, three, and then sprung from his hiding place and brought the hickory selfbow to full draw.

Echo's dad jumped back and yelled, "IT'S ME, ECHO! DON'T SHOOT!"

23

LOGAN

Saturday, October 16th

3:42 p.m.

At the sight of his dad, Echo dropped his bow and hobbled as fast as he could to reach him. Big tears streamed down each of their faces as they embraced. Finally, Echo's dad released his grip so that he could have a look at his son. "You look injured. Are you okay? What happened to you, Echo?" Ted Orion looked at Echo's injured foot and ran his fingers over the purple wounds on his neck. "Echo, what on earth happened?" repeated his dad in an anxious voice. "Why didn't you call us on the two-way radio?"

"It's a long story, Dad," said Echo. "I have so much to tell you. I got hurt when I fell out of a tree, and the radio got shattered to bits."

Looking puzzled and a little unsatisfied with Echo's answer, Ted said, "You didn't stick to the plan, Echo. We have been looking everywhere for you. We were worried sick!" With this last thought, Ted pulled a two-way radio from his pocket and shouted into it, "Olivia, do you read me?"

Echo's mom replied in a scratchy, tense voice. "Yes, Ted, I hear you. What is it?"

Shouting excitedly into the radio again, Ted said, "Come quickly. I found Echo. He is okay. Walk east down the ridge toward Young Woman's Creek. I'll blow the whistle so you can find us."

Anticipating the grilling that would come next, Echo went to his shelter to retrieve the elk hide bundle that he'd discovered at the boulder shrine. Echo expected to find an unhappy Ted Orion when he returned, but instead his dad was all smiles. "I'm so happy to see you, son," his dad said. "And proud, too. Look at this. You could survive a year in this shelter. Did you shoot that eight-point buck? If surviving this experience does not make you a Sure Enough Mountain Man, I'm not sure what will!"

Just then, they heard exited yells and splashing as Echo's mom charged across the creek to reach him. From twenty feet away, Oliva Orion screamed, "You're hurt, Echo Orion, I can see it in your face." She wrapped Echo in an enormous hug and didn't let him go until Echo nudged her away. She held his dirty face in her hands and shook her head in a way that showed she was relieved that he was safe, but was a little vexed by his careless actions too.

Noticing the elk hide bundle, Echo's mom said, "What is that? It looks old. Luna told us you might have come here to look for some kind of secret Lenape book. Is that true? Is the book in that bundle?"

Echo looked a little stunned and asked, "Why were you talking to Luna?"

How do you think we found you?" said Echo's dad. "Luna saved your tail. After we searched along the trail without finding you, Luna told us all about the clue and the book and said that you might be somewhere near Young Woman's Creek. We set off looking early this morning, and I guess Luna was right, because here you are."

Echo held up the bundle, and with a satisfied smile said, "I found this buried under a painted rock in a sort of shrine a couple hundred yards from here." Echo pointed in the direction of the shrine and started rattling off details about turtle symbols, fresh paint, and a Lenape woman riding an elk, but his dad halted Echo's speech with a forceful gesture like that of a crossing guard. "Stop, Echo! Start from the beginning and tell us what happened."

With his belt knife, Echo sliced pieces of venison from the spitted deer leg roasting over the fire. He handed several pieces of the hot meat to his parents and gestured for them to sit around the fire. Echo told them EVERYTHING: all about how he solved the clue to the hidden book, how he veered off the trail to search for the book, how he shot a grouse and fell from the big white pine, how he found the boulder shrine and the bundle by following the turtle symbols, and how he was nearly killed by a vicious pack of coyotes. Finally, he told them about the fresh paint in the boulder shrine and that he thought someone else might know about Luna's secret book and could even be watching them right now.

When Echo finished talking, Ted and Olivia Orion looked astonished. It was hard to imagine that all of this was true. They had a million questions, but before they could ask any of them, Echo reached into his coat pocket and said, "I almost forgot about this." He pulled out the mussel-shell box, but was surprised to find that it was broken open. It must have gotten smashed when he belly-crawled toward the coyotes earlier that morning.

In a soft, barely audible tone, Echo's mom said, "What is that, Echo?"

But Echo didn't answer. He was too focused on what fell from the box. Inside was an old piece of newspaper clipping, aged to the color of a dead leaf and folded into a rectangle so that it fit neatly into the box.

Echo gently unfolded the paper and began reading it aloud. "The headline says, 'After Tense Standoff, Band of Indians Forced from Their Village on Young Woman's Creek.'"

"Oh my gosh!" exclaimed Echo's mom. "Does it have a date?"

"Hold on . . . let me see," said Echo. "Yes, here it is. April 9th, 1865." Lost in his thoughts, Echo went on reading a couple of paragraphs without saying anything.

Ted Orion finally piped up anxiously, "Don't just leave us standing here, Echo. Tell us what it says!"

Echo summarized what he had just read. "It says that for as long as anyone can remember, a group of Indians and some White family members, known as the Elk Eater Band, had been living in a small village on Young Woman's Creek. With the railroad coming to the nearby town of Renovo, the Philadelphia and Erie Railroad Company had been trying to move the Indians for several years. The Indians did not want to give up their homes, saying that they had already been forced to leave their first homeland more than 150 years ago by the 'Great White Chief.'"

"The conflict grew violent when a man named James Von Ehrlich led a raiding party of railroad workers to oust the Indians at gunpoint. Von Ehrlich was building a hotel in Renovo and feared no one would visit if there were Indians and Indian lovers living nearby. A tribal chief named Elk Tongue and his granddaughter, who was called Teal Eye, were killed in the raid."

"That's horrible," cried Oliva. "Where did the Elk Eater Band go?"

"It doesn't say," said Echo. "It only says that the raiding party burned all of their bark houses and no members of the band were permitted to return."

"So, they just up and disappeared?" asked Oliva.

"I guess so," replied Echo.

"This is fascinating," said Ted, "but we need to get ourselves out of this forest. Olivia, do you remember seeing that logging road at the top of the ridge?"

"Yes, I remember it, Ted," answered Olivia.

"Great. How far do you think it is?" asked Ted.

Olivia grimaced as she mentally calculated the distance. Finally, she said, "I'd say it's at least a mile of steep uphill hiking."

Ted turned to Echo. "Son, do you think you can make the climb?"

Echo looked down at his injured foot and began talking. "It's much better than it was yesterday. The swelling is down and I can wear a boot now. I think I can make it if I have some help on the steep parts."

Now it seemed that drill sergeant dad was back, shouting orders. "Okay, here's the plan," he said in an authoritative voice. "Olivia, you hike to the logging road and then out to the hard-top road. I saw a house there with ATVs parked in the yard. See if you can get someone to bring an ATV back on the logging road to haul Echo out. Also, call Leo when you get cell signal and have him hike in with a frame pack to retrieve this deer meat and Echo's gear. Echo, we are going to take some food, water, and that elk hide bundle and begin making our way to the logging road. I suspect it will take us a while."

Only an hour of daylight remained when Ted and Echo reached the logging road. Their progress was slowed by Echo's struggle to climb the steep slope. Eventually, they worked out a technique where Echo sat on his butt, facing downhill. With a rope tied around Echo's waist, his Dad pulled him, while Echo "crab-walked" backwards on his hands and one good leg.

Soon after reaching the logging road, they heard the whine of an ATV coming. Echo smiled at his dad with relief and the two high-fived. Driving the ATV was a man they didn't recognize, and riding in a large utility cart being towed by the machine was Echo's mom, wearing a concerned look.

With an unwelcome tone and an expression of suspicion on his face, the man said, "My name is Logan. I will get you out of here. But we musn't delay. Soon darkness will come." Ted cocked his head and shot Olivia a worried look. Something wasn't right about this guy, yet when Olivia knocked on his door, he had readily agreed to help.

Logan was tall, thin, and angular in his build. He wore a grimy camouflage baseball cap that was so old, the fabric had begun to fray from the brim. Pulled back under the hat was a mane of glossy black hair that hung to the center of his back. He wore ragged work pants, like the kind that construction workers wear, and an old-school wool hunting coat of red and black plaid. The largest Bowie knife Echo had ever seen hung from Logan's hip. He was not old, nor young. Echo figured he was maybe thirty-five or forty.

Logan pointed to the cart and gestured roughly for Echo to get in. Echo's dad helped him into the cart and placed his backpack with the elk hide bundle in it beside him. Echo sat backwards, with his back against the front rail of the cart and his arms extended onto the side rails, like he was in a beach chair. When Logan bent to close the cart's tailgate, all that black hair slid to one side. Echo felt the blood drain from his face, and his stomach knotted. On Logan's neck, hidden behind all that beautiful hair, was a red tattoo. A perfect red tattoo of the Lenape turtle symbol.

Logan saw that Echo's gaze was fixed on his tattoo, but he gave no reaction. He calmly pulled his hair over his neck to cover the tattoo and said, "We must be going now."

Going where? thought Echo. His mind flashed to the trail camera outside of the boulder shrine. *This guy has a picture of me. He knows I was in his sacred place, messing with his sacred stuff. He might even know that the elk hide bundle is in this backpack right beside me. He is going to drive us deeper into the forest, chop us to bits, and leave Ole One Ear and his gang to devour the evidence.* Just then, the ATV lurched forward and they were on their way.

Ted, Olivia, and Echo sat in uncomfortable silence as the cart bounced down the logging road. Soon Echo began to see signs of human life: a seasonal cabin, a few houses tucked in the woods, and then, at last, they were at the hard-topped road. Logan turned left onto an ATV trail that ran next to the road and drove them several miles to their truck. He did not get off his ATV and only said goodbye with a stiff wave of his hand. Echo felt deep worry in the pit of his stomach as he watched Logan ride away.

24

A NEW BEGINNING

Saturday, October 23rd

12:00 p.m.

Logan stared at the fuzzy image on his computer screen. He was convinced that the boy in the photo from the trail camera was the same boy he had just rescued from the forest. Logan had made sure to ask the boy's family who they were and where they lived. His sloppy, handwritten note next to the computer said, "Ted and Olivia Orion from the Black Moshannon area." *This should be enough information*, he thought. It was time to tell the others. Logan went to the wall and lifted the receiver of an old-fashioned landline telephone.

***

The doctor in the emergency room said that Echo was lucky not to have broken any of the larger bones in his leg, like the femur or tibia. As it was, Echo's fibula bone was broken and the ankle joint badly sprained. The doctor had looked Echo in the eye while his parents stood close by and said, "You should be more careful, young man. Falls from that height can result in a broken femur, which you would not have survived without immediate medical attention. I suggest you stay out of the woods and take up something safer, like video games." Echo looked at his parents, and they all broke out in wide grins. Some people just didn't understand.

To be on the safe side, they kept Echo in the hospital for two nights to make sure there was no internal infection brewing in his ankle. It wasn't so bad. The highly processed hospital food was terrible, but they fed him three times a day, and Echo ordered tons of snacks in between. He especially liked the little cups of chocolate pudding!

The staff took a shine to Echo and often gathered around his bed to hear his stories. They liked hearing the part about how Echo ate chipmunks to survive and how Ole One Ear had nearly ripped out his throat in a fight over a deer. Echo was always cautious to never mention anything about the turtle symbol, or boulder shrine, or anything connected to his search for the Lenape book.

Ted Orion had sent word to Luna that Echo was okay and would soon be coming home. He also mentioned that Echo had a special surprise for her. Echo could not wait to give her the elk hide bundle and show her the old newspaper clipping that had been in the mussel-shell box.

But on his first day home from the hospital, his worst fears came true. After checking to make sure his natural history collection was okay, Echo grabbed his iPad to send

Buster a message. A pop-up notification on the screen said, "You have a new message from Logan3Crows." Echo began to sweat profusely as his finger hovered over the notification box. He nervously tapped the icon and read the message silently to himself. "We want what you stole from us. We are good people and will not harm you if you give back to us what is rightfully ours. We know where you live. We will be there at noon sharp on Saturday."

Echo had not told his parents about the trail camera or the tattoo he saw on Logan's neck. He was hoping that part of his adventure would just go away. But now, Logan3Crow's message gave him no choice but to confess what he knew.

Echo's parents considered calling the police, but figured that might just complicate the problem, especially for Luna. They worried that someone in law enforcement would be obligated to confiscate the elk hide bundle. Instead, Ted and Oliva decided that it would be best for Echo to tell Luna the whole story, and together they could figure out what to do next.

The reunion between Echo and Luna was tense at first. They sat at Luna's kitchen table, but unlike most times, there was no slice of homemade pie or hot coffee, just a bare wood table. She clearly had something to get off her mind and lit into Echo right off the bat. "Child, I'm happy to see you safe, but what you did was plain foolish," Luna said in a harsh tone. "And I feel responsible, giving you that clue and puttin' some wild goose chase in your head. You promised me that you wouldn't search for the book alone. Then you went and got yourself nearly killed. You risked your neck for nothin'. I'm beginning to think that book is only a myth just like everyone says."

Echo stood from his chair to make a point. "There's where you're wrong, Luna," Echo said in a sturdy, assertive voice. "I know I showed poor judgement, and I know I broke my promise to you. But if you just listen, I think you'll change your mind on some things." Echo sat back down and began unreeling his story, from finding the first turtle symbol to the crazy message from Logan3Crows.

Luna was dumbfounded and sat in silence as Echo told his story. When he finished, she said only four words: "Where is the bundle?" Excitement like Echo had never seen before danced in the old woman's eyes when Echo pulled the elk hide bundle from his backpack. "Oh, thank you, child, thank you, child!" she cried.

Luna reached for a knife to cut the bundle's sinew wrappings. She'd waited her whole life for this and wasn't going to waste another second. But Echo yelled, "No, stop! Think about it, Luna. It's not that simple. We have to deal with Logan3Crows first. We have to keep the peace or whatever is wrapped in that elk hide might be lost for another one hundred fifty years. We can't let that happen. We—no, *you*, more than anyone—need the truth."

Together, they made a plan. Or, in Luna's case, it was more of a pact. Luna promised that she would not open the elk hide bundle. Instead, she would keep it just as Echo had found it and bring it to the meeting with Logan3Crows on Saturday. She would also bring the first Lenape Book of Ways left to her by her mother, and the deerskin jacket with the turtle symbol on the back that Echo had seen in Luna's cabin. Luna would present Logan3Crows with her own sacred Lenape items to convince him that her ancestral connections to the Lenape people were authentic, and that she had a right to whatever was wrapped in that elk hide bundle.

On Saturday morning, the Orions' cabin was thick with nervous energy. Echo paced like a tiger in a cage, Ted pretended to catch up on the news, and Olivia brought in the last of the winter squash from the garden. The only one who didn't seem nervous was Rachel. She was excited to see this whole thing go down and busied herself making coffee and snacks for their guests . . . or enemies . . . or whomever these people were.

At eleven thirty, Luna's old truck pulled up the driveway. If it hadn't been for the truck, Echo might not have recognized the person who stepped out of it. In place of her usual denim overalls, Luna wore a dress made of tan deerskin that was cinched at the waist with a buffalo skin belt. The dress was fringed where it stopped just above her knees and was decorated all over with intricate red and black beadwork. Her shiny black-and-gray hair was pulled into a single, thick braid that hung to the center of her back. Around her throat was a choker-style necklace made of porcupine quills and colorful wampum beads.

"Wow! You look GREAT," said Echo when Luna stepped down from the truck.

"Oh, stop it, child," was all Luna said in reply. Luna handed Echo the unopened elk hide bundle, the Book of Lenape Ways, and the deerskin jacket to be hidden until they could get a read on Logan3Crows. There was no sense in showing their cards until they knew who they were dealing with.

At noon sharp, a black SUV with tinted windows and red-clay mud splashed down its sides pulled up the driveway. Echo's dad insisted everyone stay inside while he confronted these people on his own. Echo and Luna watched from a window inside the cabin as Logan, the same man who had driven them from the forest in the utility cart, stepped from the SUV. Logan wore the same sour look and the same intimidating Bowie knife on his belt. Echo could tell from their stiff postures and erratic hand gestures that the conversation between his dad and Logan was tense and unfriendly. Echo kept a close eye on Logan's hand that was nearest the Bowie knife. When Logan began angrily pointing his finger in Ted Orion's face, Luna stormed from the cabin and into the driveway.

The appearance of the old woman in her deerskin dress halted the conversation as Logan tried to make sense of it all. But before another word could be breathed, the rear door of the SUV swung open violently, causing Echo to gasp from inside the cabin. "What's happening?" yelled Rachel from the kitchen.

From the SUV stepped a very old man who looked remarkably similar to Luna, with the same tall, angular build and chiseled facial features. The old man's hair was the color of a new baseball and it fell in great wisps to the tops of his shoulders. He wore red pants made of lightweight, homespun wool. These were tucked into knee-high moccasins built from buckskin and intricately decorated with red and black beads. A single Bald Eagle feather hung from a leather thong around his wrinkled neck.

But, amazingly, those were not the most striking features about the old man. On his top half, he wore an old deerskin jacket with the Lenape turtle symbol stitched onto the back in gorgeous red beads. To Echo's eye, the jacket looked identical to the one Luna had.

"Holy cow! He has the same jacket as Luna," hollered Echo. "This is legit. Mom, Rachel, come here and see this!"

Outside in the driveway, it seemed the world had stopped. No one spoke. No one moved. Ted Orion stared, dumbfounded, at the old man, while Logan and the old man gave Luna a shocked but satisfied look of recognition.

Finally, the old man made the first move. He was surprisingly spry and went directly to Luna, stopping only inches from her face. Echo made it to the driveway in time to hear the old man say to Luna in a slow, warm voice, "I am Chief Soaring Eagle, descended from the great Chief Bald Eagle. You are the lost one. But you are no longer alone. My blood is your blood. The Elk Eaters have been waiting all these years. Welcome home." Luna changed before their eyes. The years of grief that had accumulated on her face fell away and was replaced by happiness. She stood proud, seeming now to understand her place in the world. Soaring Eagle pulled Luna into a big hug, and the two shed silent tears, which washed over their deerskins like rain giving life for a new tree to grow where an old one had just died.

When Soaring Eagle released Luna from his tremendous grip, she turned immediately to Echo, dropping low to look him in the eyes. In a voice choked with emotion and barely above a whisper, Luna said, "When the seed of the oak grows into a mighty tree, towering above all others, we can no longer call it an acorn. Same as the acorn outgrows its name, I can no longer call you 'child.' Thank you, Echo Orion, for closing my circle, for making me whole again."

Pride and happiness swelled in Echo's heart. No more words were needed. It was clear as the bugle from a bull elk on a frosty autumn morning. Echo had become a Sure Enough Mountain Man indeed.

EPILOGUE

LUNA AND THE ELK EATER BAND

After being forced from their village on Young Woman's Creek in 1865, the Lenape Elk Eater Band secretly slipped into the surrounding area. They lived in conventional houses at the edge of town and deep in the forest. The Band was already a mixture of Indians and Whites, and as time went on, they accepted more trusted Whites into their families as husbands and wives. Luna had become cut off from her ancestors when her mother, who at just sixteen, left the Band over a dispute with her father, who was the Band's chief. Luna's mother wanted the Band to be less secretive and become more integrated with the White community, but the Band did not agree. When she ran away, Luna's mother left behind a twin sister, who was Chief Soaring Eagle's mother, making Luna and Soaring Eagle first cousins.

Over the years, the Band continued to practice sacred ceremonies at the boulder shrine and they waited for the "lost one" to return by following the clue left behind in the Lenape Book of Ways.

Since the killing of Chief Bald Eagle in 1779, the Lenape had been living under the "Prophecy of the Fourth Crow." The Prophecy of the Fourth Crow tells the story of how the Lenape people have struggled to survive and keep their community and culture together. The First Crow represents the Lenape before the coming of the Whites to their native homeland on the Mid-Atlantic Coast. The Second Crow symbolizes the death and destruction of Lenape culture. The Third Crow represents the Lenape going into hiding. The Fourth Crow is the Lenape becoming caretakers again and working with everybody to restore land, community, and culture. The painting on the center rock in the boulder shrine had only three crows, as it was created under The Third Crow, or what was known as the time of hiding.

Upon Luna's return to the Band, she taught the Elk Eaters that many Whites, like the Orions, were good people and accepting of Native American heritage. The Band agreed that the time of the Fourth Crow had come, and they began emerging to rebuild their community.

Echo and the Orions

Soon after recovering from his Sure Enough Mountain Man adventure, Echo passed the state Hunter's Safety Course and went on to hunt with his family that fall. His knowledge about natural history, wilderness survival, and native cultures continued to grow. After writing an engaging essay about his experience for his history class at school, Echo's teacher asked him to tell his story in a special assembly at the end of the school year. He titled it "A Sure Enough Mountain Man Learns a Few Lessons." It was a huge hit and made Ted and Olivia very proud of their son.

Upon hearing Echo's story about being visited by a crow while at the boulder shrine and when facing down Ole One Ear, Chief Soaring Eagle said that in the tradition of the Lenape Vision Quest, Echo's spirit animal was the crow. After a council vote, Echo was accepted into the Elk Eater Band and was given the Lenape name, "Brave Crow."

About the Author

Ron Rohrbaugh is a professional wildlife biologist and author who spent more than twenty-five years at Cornell University and the National Audubon Society. He has published dozens of feature articles in outdoor magazines. His other books include, *A Traditional Bowhunter's Path*, which has won praise for its engaging storytelling and focus on the critical role that hunters play as conservationists. Ron is the owner of LifeCycle Gear, which focuses on making and selling quality traditional archery equipment. He is a member of the Pennsylvania Outdoor Writers Association and lives with his wife, Debbie, and two young children in a log cabin on the Allegheny Front in North Central Pennsylvania.

For more information, contact RonRohrbaugh@gmail.com.

Connecting and Reviewing

I hope you have enjoyed this book and have been inspired to go camping, start a natural history collection, try hunting or fishing, or build a survival shelter in your backyard.

I'd love to hear about your outdoor adventures. You can share them with me and other LIVING WILD book fans by using the hashtag #smartsandways on social media.

Online reviews are critically important for authors like me, and for helping others to discover the books you love. If you enjoyed this book, I'd be very grateful if could provide a review at the website where you made your purchase and on social media.

Thank You!

Ron

Made in the USA
Las Vegas, NV
16 October 2023

79154336R00104